Published by Semiotext(e)
PO BOX 629, South Pasadena, CA 91031
www.semiotexte.com

Translation Copyright © Jacob Steinberg, 2021

"Congreso, 1994," "Dear Timo," "Fat Cat Records (or a Cloud with the Color and Shape of a Bruise)," "Dear Kathrin," "Flourishing Peach II," "Unlimited Budget," "Nuns, the Utopia of a World Without Men," and "A Post-Marxist Theory of Unhappiness" were previously published, in modified form, in Licorice Candies by Scrambler Books in 2016.

Cover: Julie Becker, *I am am I?*, 2010. Mixed media. 17 1/8 x 14 inches (43.5 x 35.6 cm). Courtesy of Greene Naftali, New York

Design: Hedi El Kholti
ISBN: 978-1-63590-140-5

Distributed by the MIT Press, Cambridge, MA, and London, England.
Printed and bound in the United States of America.

Cecilia Pavón

Little Joy

Selected Stories

Translated by Jacob Steinberg

semiotext(e)

Contents

Congreso, 1994   7

Dear Timo   10

Types of Plastic   11

Fat Cat Records, or a Cloud with the Color and Shape of a Bruise   16

Autopoiesis (1999)   21

Dear Kathrin   25

Trisha Erin   27

Dear Johanna   35

Sergio and I   37

Every Picture I Ever Threw Away   41

Swedenborg vs. Kant   46

Losing Weight   54

Flourishing Peach II   59

Unlimited Budget   65

Jeans   71

Every Bag I've Ever Owned   86

A Bottle of Vichy Makeup Remover I Stole from a Poet in Berlin   96

Easily Amused   103

Noelle Kocot	106
I Want to Be Fat	112
Nuns, the Utopia of a World without Men	116
A Post-Marxist Theory of Unhappiness	122
Michelle Mattiuzzi	133
The Gray Journal	138
Amalia Ulman (A Happy Week)	141
Do It Yourself	146
What Is a Poem?	152
The Flawed Concept of Coupledom	156
Freestyle Rap	160
Two Stories about Downtown Buenos Aires	167
Untitled	174
Little Joy (Temporary Autonomous Zone)	176
Dreams Can't Be Copyrighted	181
A Perfect Day	184
Diary of a Cloud Watcher	192

Congreso, 1994

I just moved to Buenos Aires. I only really know the three blocks between my apartment building and the club. I haven't gone to Palermo yet, I don't know where San Isidro is or how to even get there, and I haven't been to Devoto or Pompeya. On Thursday nights, I walk my three blocks in ecstasy.

I live in Congreso. My aunt, who moved to Buenos Aires thirty years ago, also lives in Congreso. Whenever any of my aunts, uncles, sisters, brothers, or cousins come to Buenos Aires, they stay in Congreso. Congreso is the neighborhood for people from the provinces. Maybe this is how people from the provinces envision the city: full of offices and devoid of children. Congreso is an impersonal neighborhood, and yet, all the best nightclubs in Buenos Aires are in Congreso. On Thursday nights, I walk down a narrow, dimly lit street on my way to the club. I don't know anybody, but I go anyways. I stand in the middle of the dance floor and move with my eyes closed.

There's nothing quite like crossing 9 de Julio Avenue at 5 a.m., when it's empty. Its vastness and emptiness are the closest things you'll find to the countryside.

Some Thursdays, when it's still too early to go out dancing and I haven't got anything to do (honestly, I almost never have anything to do), I sit at a café on Avenida de Mayo to have a drink—cider or champagne. I always choose the table closest to the street. The noise from the cars is deafening, but I close my eyes and pretend it's the sea.

Ever since moving to Buenos Aires, that's all I've really done: mentally superimpose nature on the city. Congreso is the perfect neighborhood for superimposing nature on the city. Walking along Hipólito Irigoyen Street on dark, poorly lit nights is like walking through a forest. The dry plazas and uneven sidewalks are just like the wilderness of the Andes.

Other than the club I go to, what I love most about this neighborhood is its frequent blackouts. When all the household appliances stop working—and the elevator, too—I run down the nine flights of stairs separating me from the ground floor. I open the door and run to the plaza across the street. When the lights go out, the city becomes like a cave, and the light from the cars becomes the beating of a chaotic, arrhythmic heart. A heart that is deformed, monstrous, like the sounds of the city.

I like living in Congreso because there are nightclubs, and I like going to the club because I think of it as a school. I don't go to the club to meet men or feel the music in my body or drink exotic cocktails. I go just to reeducate my ears. After incorporating the arrangement of the unfamiliar music they play there into my system of perception, the sounds of the street become like music to me. Then, I no longer suffer. Whenever I feel like that noise is wounding my soul, I say, "It's not wounding it. It's giving it joy. Noise is pleasure, like Daft Punk's music." Furthermore, that noise is always with me. Thanks to that noise, I never feel alone in Congreso. Whenever I go anywhere, I never feel like I'm walking on asphalt, but rather on a mattress of noises or a carpet whose pattern is an intricate blend of mysterious, exciting sounds.

Really, this is all I can say about Congreso: My body is motionless in my apartment, and the only movement is that of the sounds. (Wind, radios that blend with buses and ambulances, drills, TV sets, people shouting just for the hell of it, or people shouting political slogans to the beat of powerful drums.)

And lastly, I don't want to live in a Buenos Aires apartment; I want to live in a Buenos Aires nightclub. Or better yet: I don't want to live; I want to dance. Actually, I don't want to dance, I just want to listen, listen, listen.

Dear Timo

Last night, I got drunk, and when I went to bed and closed my eyes, I envisioned my body moving, just because, along a horizontal path. Continually, on a horizontal path, for thousands and thousands of miles. First, it reached the Argentine border at the coast of the Río de la Plata. Then it went on and on, crossing the sea... And then, my thoughts paused, wondering... Had I reached Africa? As you can tell, I don't understand real geography at all. (Sometimes I don't know which country on the map is Peru, where Ecuador is, or if Mexico is in South America or on Mars.) In reality, more than a question, it was a wish. I wished that, by continually moving like that along a straight path, my body could make it to Germany... That you could reach Berlin from Buenos Aires in an instant without any airplanes. That the world's coolest cities were each an extension of the next: Lima, Buenos Aires, Berlin. All next to one another, reachable by intercity bus (one of those ones with on-board movies and coffee carts). Don't you think that would be just great, given how often you cross the ocean, following birds' migratory patterns, just always in the wrong direction?

Types of Plastic

I hope I never become a writer who hoards, a consumer; a writer with brand new towels and sheets at home, who throws out any clothes they have worn too many times from their closet. One of those people who can't stand discolored dishcloths with stains from meals they made months or even years ago—stains from peaches, raw meat, or kitchen grease. By definition, a writer must prefer gender-neutral pronouns rather than female ones, and further, they must have worn-out towels with blood or bleach stains, and the same sheets as forever ago with elastic edges too stretched out to fit the mattress anymore. To write is to accept the wear and tear of objects. Poetry is like rust, impossibly orange stains that slowly corrode the spine of life. I've meditated on this for years: Life only exists to be consumed by poetry, like an iron pole knocked down by the mystery of rust.

It's too cold for this time of year; it feels like fall. I am holed up at home watching Instagram accounts and trying to envision the future—or to be more specific, *my* future. On the TV in the living room, they're saying it's snowing in Patagonia. Snow? In January? The heart of summer?

Last night I had a very strange dream: I came across every object I've ever thrown away from as far back as I can remember.

I'm not talking about food scraps or shapeless things like dust or wood splinters, but rather all those other objects, things that could have still been useful for something but I threw away because I didn't have anywhere to store them or didn't really know what to do with them: plastic bags; hundreds, thousands of me and my son's toys; garden chairs; fake fur coats; cooking oil and shampoo bottles… Like in a Borgesian Aleph—biographical and partial—somebody or something brought me to my building's boiler room in the basement, where it showed me a small, luminous circumference containing every object I ever threw away that still had some use or could have been given away. Upon seeing them all, I felt a strong sense of nostalgia for some of the items and wished I could get them back. Although maybe it wasn't really nostalgia, but guilt. (For example, a miniature porcelain tea set that my grandmother gave me in San Juan in 1978, which, when I moved out on my own for the first time in 1990, I left in a light-blue bag in a garbage can at my parent's house.) Then I stretched out my hand toward that luminous sphere that contained the totality of my discarded possessions. At that point, everything faded away, and after a few seconds of a kind of silvery, sticky darkness, I was in a completely different scene. Now, I was an 11-year-old girl living in a wooden house in Sumatra. We were near the Java Sea, just next to the shore, and probably from the humidity and salt, several of the planks making up the walls of my home were weathered. In the dream, I knew with complete certainty that I was poor, but happy. I only ate whatever the members of my extended family fished. My house (which felt like a palace to me) was surrounded by an enormous floating tapestry, an irregular, multicolored one that grew bigger by the day and stretched out into the sea, creating new streets over the ocean I could walk on—something that blew my mind and I couldn't get over. I had never gone to school, so I didn't have even the slightest idea that plastic degraded slowly, its molecules ending up in the stomachs of jellyfish and turtles, animals I loved. Because of my ignorance, the fact that ocean currents had brought all those old, worn-out plastic objects to my house felt like a kind of miracle to me. Everything was beautiful and apocalyptic in this second part of the dream. I would have liked it if all that garbage had continued piling up until I could reach the middle of the ocean by foot, but unfortunately some noise in the house woke me up before sunrise. (My teenage son doesn't go to bed until 6 am.)

Since waking up a few hours ago, I've been in bed, phone in hand, scrolling through social media posts. Could social media and poetry somehow be connected? In a sense, they are like motionless journeys. Thanks to social media (through something a friend of a friend sent me), I fell in love with an artist from London: Linda Ruppart. They keep their head shaved and are overweight; they have a cat and a boyfriend who looks gay; and they use gender-neutral pronouns. In an Instagram story, they said they were angry with a professor at their art school who refused to call them "they." In Spanish, we don't have an existing third-person pronoun to refer to gender-neutral people. What a shame. I've felt gender-neutral since I'm 7. I think that was when I wrote my first poem to the sun and lost my feminine identity (to put it one way), even though I continue wearing women's clothes, which is what I prefer. Linda Ruppart is a visual artist, but their work is made up almost entirely of texts. They just published two volumes: a science fiction book and a book of poems. Their poetry, titled *Waiting in Line for Death*, has a ritual before each poem that the poem itself is part of, as if to say, "Writing a poem and publishing it on a blank page (or on a screen) isn't enough; you must do something else." On page 24 they talk about a ritual to heal the Earth. "It's too late," they write, "but we can still try."

Yesterday, before going to bed, I was reading a pdf of it on my computer, because Linda posted it to download for free. Then came my dream with all those objects, the plastic, Sumatra, and the ocean. Now that I'm thinking about it, that dream was how Linda's book got into my blood and became a ritual poem signed by me.

It's 12:30 p.m. on a Sunday in January, I'm rushing out of my apartment and running to the new park they just opened two blocks away, at the corner of Moreno and Jujuy. I stop in front of a kind of small, grass mountain, and with all the force of my lungs, I recite my new poem:

ONE, polyethylene terephthalate,
TWO, high-density polyethylene,
THREE, polyvinyl chloride,
FOUR, low-density polyethylene,
FIVE, polypropylene,
SIX, polystyrene.
Types of plastic, types of plastic, types of plastic.

It's a rather simple poem, but I repeat it over and over for hours. People come over, stand around me, and listen. Some clap, others hug me, most of them don't understand what I'm doing.

Types of plastic, types of plastic, types of plastic.

I keep repeating it, as though possessed by a force I neither understand nor choose. Suddenly, everything plastic around me and everybody else in the park (my spectators) goes through some kind of chemical process, accelerating its conversion to petroleum, that's to say all the plastics reverted back to the material used to make them. So, so many plastic things become black liquid (trash cans, water bottles, purses, shoes) that, suddenly, this beautiful park is no longer green. It becomes a dark, viscous pond.

Fat Cat Records, or a Cloud with the Color and Shape of a Bruise

I am the owner, founder, and sole investor in the record label Discos Gato Gordo. I stole the name from an underground British label, Fat Cat Records. My business goal is to capture the latest sounds, that is, to promote Buenos Aires's experimental musicians.

But is what they make even music? I started the business with such high hopes, but now I've come to realize how hard it is to deal with this market's obstacles. Is it actually hard to fight against the obstacles in this market? Or am I just not good at my job?

My head's full of doubts, and it's spinning like a top as I watch ships pass by. Cargo ships—who knows what they'll bring or take. (My office is on the thirtieth floor of a building near the Río de la Plata.) Ah, the river air! It's the only thing that invigorates me as I *fight* with them, the artists. Although the reason I *started* this business was just to be in contact with them.

We've already released three albums that are selling pretty well, and they've helped me recover some of the capital I invested. But it's getting harder and harder to promote the people I work with. Electronic music has its limits: They don't love it just anywhere, the clientele disappears quickly, and the market is so small. Particularly now that Latino music is all the rage in Buenos Aires. Buenos Aires—which used to be so cosmopolitan, but slowly seems to be losing its features, forgetting its identity. Though perhaps it's just a transformation like any other. Cumbia villera, a kind of bad imitation of gangsta rap, is spreading at an unthinkable rate, leaving a diminished playing field in its wake for avant-garde producers like me.

All in all, it's not like artists releasing physical CDs (all the records I've produced have been made exclusively on computers) are easy to manage either. And as I already mentioned, they also aren't easy to sell. It's music without an edge: monotonous, instrumental, bodiless, faceless, and genderless. (The music videos consist of nothing more than animated, colorful geometric shapes.) But it's the future, even if most people don't get it. So I'll push forward with my project. But if even the artists themselves don't get it... I mean, get it? They don't get it—nor should they. (Should music emerge from reflection?) It just pains me to see how they're a product of the same alienation that holds our company back from growing. They make this kind of music, but they're also at odds with it. It's so strange, and hard for me to define. Maybe it has to do with the environment. There's a saying—I think I read it in a book—"Your city is your mind." My artists all live in Buenos Aires or its suburbs, Greater Buenos Aires. A megalopolis of the so-called third world, which, then again, doesn't necessarily mean that it can't produce a unique, vital (in other words, "original") sound that can attract worldwide attention.

Buenos Aires isn't a particularly beautiful city. Green spaces have shrunken from 183 sq. ft. per person in 1912 to just 43 in 2002. The World Health Organization recommends about 140 for a respectable quality of life. We live in a cement tapestry, a thicket of asphalt, which is growing by the day without oversight or urban planning. Or at least that's what we think, because with the whole external debt crisis, the parks and recreation officials haven't prioritized keeping the public up to date on their work. Just today, for instance, there was a forest fire in the Ecological Reserve, that patch of greenery you come across just before the brown, muddy riverbank of the Río de la Plata, which hasn't been integrated into the city in any beautiful or meaningful way (like how the Limmat crosses Zurich or the Rhine crosses Cologne). They're saying the fire was an act of arson by overzealous real estate developers who want to literally clear the way for the privatization of the property so they can build their grand glass towers with pools and private spas. Buenos Aires isn't a beautiful city, because we live, quite clearly, on the savage side of capitalism.

A cloud of black smoke crossed the sky today. We saw it from the office. Its ashes made it all the way downtown. Marisa Berquis and I were in the middle of listening to her latest demo, and there it showed up—that cloud with the color and shape of a bruise. Initially, we didn't know whether to laugh or to cry. While neither of us said it, we both thought it was probably something toxic: a war, an attack, or an explosion at some run-down factory. But at the same time, there was something fascinating about the way the mass cleared a path, painting absurd shapes in the sky in just fractions of a second. It was exciting, because it was strange… and big. And it was in the sky. How can I describe the vibe it created when that image combined with the music in the background?

"It's hot, thick, sticky music, like the hot wax they drip on your thighs as you get ready for summer," Marisa said, and right away, that hot, sticky wax overtook the sky. And we were frozen.

And by this, I'm not trying to say that the music I promote has that kind of effect: paralyzing people in place. Not at all. Some might read it that way, of course, but those are just cumbia villera fans, the types who love soccer stadiums.

Marisa is 23, and she lives in a 194-square-foot apartment with turquoise carpet that she says reminds her of the color of the sea. Her only furniture is a fold-up bed, and she eats on the floor. The rest of the space is filled with CDs without artwork (she downloads everything online) sprawled across the floor. The first time I walked into her place, I felt like I was inside an aquarium. (The bathroom has carpet too, and the wooden door is a bit sunken, so it doesn't close all the way, and when she showers, she uses extremely hot water, so the whole space steams up.)

I think she's one of my most important artists, and her creations excite me to the core. I like her music because it's visceral, melancholic, and light in equal proportions. When I listen to it alone with the lights off, I cry. In that regard, I think all the records I've produced should be listened to with the lights off, in total darkness.

None of my records have beats, and sometimes I like to think of them as pieces that facilitate long, introspective journeys, or trips into a dream state, as if listening to music and dying were one and the same. Just imagine if all those overwhelming masses living in poverty and listening to cumbia villera instead listened to Marisa Berquis, like hot, sticky wax, lying in the dark, without drinking or moving. What effect would it have? What would happen to our country? Or what if, instead of soccer, Sundays were set aside for mass listening sessions with ambient music in sports stadiums. Obviously, this will never happen, but I like to picture it: everybody sedated by the sticky music of Discos Gato Gordo. A totalitarian—and, still pacifist—utopia, because if there's anything I hate, it's soccer.

And I really don't need to explain that, do I? Because anybody reading this report must also hate soccer, right?

Autopoiesis (1999)

My friend Alejandro Ros, who is a famous designer from Argentina, just went to Burning Man in the Nevada Desert. I found out about his trip on Facebook, because to be honest, I haven't seen him in real life in many years. Life and responsibilities gradually pulled us in different directions. He posted amazing photos that look like they're straight out of an illustration book from the '70s. The lighting is faded; all the colors look a little burnt. I'm not sure what the right terminology is... Everything looks filtered by the light of a pink sunset. I'm sure that's what it must have felt like to be there. On the horizon, far off, you can make out the figures of a wooden man and woman just starting to catch fire. There's also a video where they're burning a wooden temple. The wind starts swirling, forming twenty-two small tornadoes of fire that look like crazed hummingbirds ablaze. I know there are exactly twenty-two; I counted them.

I watched that video at 3 a.m. as I was trying to finish a poem in the small room where I write, right next to my kitchen. There's no greater joy for me than occupying that space with my laptop open, even if I get distracted on Facebook, even if after two hours all I've done is write one letter or erased a comma: the joy of writing. Could it approximate the joy of dancing naked at Burning Man? I'm writing in a 40-square-foot room that, at some other point, must have been a space for ironing or storing cleaning supplies. Every day, after making dinner and putting my son to bed, I sit down to write about eight feet from the oven and washing machine. Fire and water. But not outdoors like at that festival, which seems distant and frozen on my laptop screen; rather, in my 730-square-foot apartment. As the city sleeps and the whole building is silent, my one-person festival starts on a blank page. For when I write, I dance on my own, and things catch fire in front of me, behind me, all around me. Like in that Billy Idol song I love, "Dancing with Myself."

According to what I read on Wikipedia, Burning Man's organizers believe fire has a cleansing power. Did my friend head to the Nevada Desert to cleanse himself? I met Alejandro at the end of the '90s, in the previous century. He always hosted parties where people took drugs and danced in a big circle. (Last century, I danced with other people in big circles.) I'll never forget those parties. They were on Thursday nights. We were all single, so we could stay as late as we wanted. In Alejandro's tiny living room, there was a white fur rug and a disco ball hanging from the ceiling. Alejandro had the best music equipment in Buenos Aires. It could produce the most precise, well-defined sound. He also had the most comprehensive, complicated, and sophisticated electronic music collection in the city. Or at least I liked to think so. On his balcony, there were just cacti and prickly pears in smooth concrete rectangular planters.

If there's any point where I seemed to be something akin to a follower of gurus, it was from 1999 to 2002. And Alejandro was my humble, vernacular guru. I learned from him that dancing is better than going to therapy. But it wasn't just any old dancing; it had to be the way we did it. We danced in a rather tender way that could induce a state of deep introspection in us. We would smoke weed and dance for three, four, five hours, and nobody was allowed to talk. It wasn't ever specified, but it was still a rule, as tacit as it was strict. Further, the apartment, by virtue of being so white and empty, felt like a temple. Later, my guru (I don't know if he was other people's guru, but he was certainly mine) would take out mint chocolate chip ice cream bars from the freezer, and we would eat them while we made ridiculous jokes, none of which I remember, obviously.

Now that I think of it, I wonder if everybody else there— Gaby, Pablo, Leo, Gary, Eze, Fer, and a lot of others, too—felt like those circle dances we did were transcendental. Maybe they experienced it all differently. Maybe for them, they were just nights of drugs and relaxation downtown in a wild metropolis. (And I add, not just any wild metropolis, but *the* wild metropolis—Buenos Aires, my city, the most delirious city on planet Earth.) In any event, does it really matter whether or not everybody else felt the same way as me? Those circle dances left their mark. They left their mark on my brain that, like a simple den animal, began to dig and dig subterranean tunnels into everything. Thursdays were my days of cleansing. Dancing made me feel like I was in this world and outside of it, all at the same time. And that was brilliant—a feeling of freedom.

I remember one time we went to the countryside, brought these small speakers, and danced, hypnotized by the frogs' croaking. "The song of the frogs is bewitching," somebody wrote in a poem after I told them about this.

Now, fifteen years later, I hardly go to parties anymore, because I stay at home watching TV or writing stories. Nonetheless, I feel like dancing proceeds down its unseen path in my spirit. And I'm not referring only to the fact that I think writing (and life) can be explained through the metaphor of dance. What I mean to say is that in those dance circles, what really happened was we all stopped being people and became objects. We erased our biography (our flesh), and for 120 minutes, which were always infinite, music let us be blank sheets floating around an apartment in Retiro...

Dear Kathrin

If there's one thing I hate about Buenos Aires, it's that people don't connect with each other when they dance. I noticed it last night, and it's terrible. Everybody dances for themselves. They practically stare at the ground the whole time. And on top of that, they're bad dancers, too. Like they're afraid of the music. And it isn't like this with the financial crisis. This attitude on the dance floor was there before. It's always been around. I can't remember even a single party where the people had good moves. Now that I've spent three weeks in Germany and had a chance to experience the Berlin nightlife, I see it clearly. They say Germans are too rigid, but they're far better dancers than Argentines. How can I explain it... It's a question of surrendering yourself to the group. Each person comes up with a move and inspires everybody else, and just like that, a kind of web starts to form, culminating in communion. I have the feeling that Argentines are afraid of being judged when they dance. For instance, they hardly move their hips. They never make eye contact with one another. They don't even come up with any choreography or try to coordinate their moves. I don't know... I'm saying this from a makeshift party that happens each Sunday at 7 p.m. in a spot on Santa Fe Avenue. The DJ is the ex-wife of a successful rock star. After the divorce, she decided to give deejaying a shot. When she went to Barcelona with her husband (for one of his shows), she bought all the new, trendy music. Because of that, she's one of the few DJs that can find work here. But it isn't fair. What's the point of having all the latest records if she can't mix well? She's ultimately just a poser. But whatever. She's the one who came back with all the music, not her ex. And that's all organizers care about when they need to book shows.

Trisha Erin

"This is a third-world shithole!" T. E. said. She didn't say it to me, but I heard about how she had said it, upset, to Alexander, the curator at the National Museum of Fine Arts. It was Alexander who brought T. E. to Buenos Aires. She was wearing a Vivienne Westwood dress that replicated the design of the British flag, though, adhering to her body's curves, the design wasn't completely apparent.

In my purse, I had a folded-up sheet of paper with a poem bearing her name as its title. I had written it as an homage and was considering giving it to her that night. It was the only thing I had in my otherwise empty purse. This was the poem:

"Trisha Erin"

Sometimes pain feels like someone has cut off your
arm, but I have a thousand arms, and a thousand legs,
and a thousand hearts.
I guess I haven't made enough of an effort in my life,
that's why I feel pain
If I were truly a solipsist, what reason would I have to
feel pain? I'd look at the moon and know that the

moon is I. The moon doesn't feel pain. It is water that feels pain. And I am water, I'm a castle of water and my entrails lie scattered across the sea.

That night, the museum had organized a dinner with T. E. in a Peruvian restaurant in Belgrano with several of the big players in the local art scene: critics, journalists, curators, gallery owners, and a few artists... The only reason they invited me was because I had translated a book of her columns, which the curator and I decided to call *Proximity to Love*. I later found out that she absolutely loved the title and the concept. Just about the only thing she said to me when I met her briefly on the night of the exhibit opening was, "I love that title. How did you come up with it?" I told her the truth, that it was something she herself had written, which I took from one of her articles where she wrote about her mother, who was nearly 80 years old, coming to her studio and making her pancakes. I think that's all we managed to say to each other. It was in the coffee shop just next to the museum, in front of a park, on the day of her exhibit's opening. It was a beautiful night, because summer had just begun to show hints of its imminent arrival. I remember a swarm of people surrounding T. E. Alex was there, as were Dalia (my artist friend) and several English women who were friends of T. E. It was the only thing I managed to say to her, but I didn't manage to even finish my sentence. She wasn't interested in hearing that the book's title had been inspired by her mother's volcanic love ("volcanic" in the sense that it's inevitable that it will overflow like lava; now that I am a mother, I understand this).

I don't think a class on love was something T. E. was expecting at that point in her life. A mother's love wasn't the right thing for T. E.'s stage of existence at the time. All Trisha thought about was getting a boyfriend. And because she was famous, she couldn't stand hearing about anything that didn't have to do with fulfilling her desire—the desire that somebody love her romantically and passionately. She simply turned around and started talking with her friends who had flown from Australia to Buenos Aires just to be with her for the show's opening. (People with money always have friends in another part of the world that fly in for their close friends' important events.) I stayed there, hands in my skirt pockets, trying to smile.

During the dinner, Trish (which is what I heard her close friends call her) seemed a little annoyed with the whole situation. They had placed me at a table quite far from hers, with other second-tier artists. The important ones (like Guillermo Kuitca), some of the art critics for the major newspapers, and the two or three important art patrons of Buenos Aires all sat at T. E.'s table. As I ate, I thought about what a huge disappointment meeting her had been. About how much I had dreamed of that moment when I translated her impassioned texts and about how evil, cold, and monstrous she seemed to me, calling Buenos Aires a "shithole." But on the other hand, I also had to admit that all 20th-century artists were kind of monsters—monsters screaming their deformity at the world in high-pitched screams. From Yves Klein, who painted women blue, to Jackson Pollock's disgusting drips and splashes (not to even mention that French artist with her gigantic spiders). Ah, and lest we forget the psychotic

Chinese artist who saw red polka dots in the sky and all around. Or was she Japanese...just to name a few. In any event, at one point in the night, Trisha Erin caused a scene because they were serving smoked salmon, and she is allergic to salmon. Distraught, the museum's PR rep left the restaurant crying, swiftly followed by the curator who went to console her. A few moments later, Trish let her head fall down on the table and passed out.

The night went on, and I still had the poem in my purse. Obviously, I didn't care about giving it to her anymore. All I wanted was for everything to wrap up as soon as possible so I could go home. Something else that crossed my mind: the amount of money I had wasted buying myself that silk, beige-colored skirt and black linen shirt for a dinner that, in the end, didn't lead to anything. When I was buying them, I fantasized about different possible scenarios: what if Trisha Erin became intrigued by my personality and decided to invite me to spend a month or two at her house in southern France to write a novel together; what if Trisha Erin fell in love with Buenos Aires's underground art scene and decided to open and finance a totally non-commercial gallery with her own money in Villa Crespo, naming me its director with a salary of five thousand pounds a month; what if Trisha Erin fell in love with my friend Javier Barilaro and proposed to him and asked me to be the witness at their wedding. Two days earlier, I was trying on every single item at a local clothing store before I picked the most appropriate outfit for the occasion. I wasted a whole afternoon and fell behind on the French theory text I'd been translating. But it had all been in vain.

What's more, I had paid for it all on my credit card with installments. Now, each month's payment would be like a dose of venom, reminding me of the night's bitterness.

Alexander came over to our table from time to time trying to appease the various groups so nobody would be upset with him. Each time the curator moved, the English artist's eyes were like two magnets fixated on his neck. The truth was Trisha was in love with Alexander, and the only thing that inspired her to come to Buenos Aires was the illusion of having a one-night stand with her curator in the Recoleta Four Seasons, where she was staying. That was the only reason she agreed to come without an appearance fee to this dreary, sad, distant country. In the end, Alex refused to sleep with her. At least that's what he told me, and I believe him. Though he was a rather shady character himself too.

While translating the book, Alexander and I wrote each other exactly 1,436 emails, according to Gmail. From his iPhone, he'd send me pictures of him and Trisha together: the two of them eating caviar in London; idyllic images of a trip they took together to the Bahamas to visit I-don't-know-which collector; pics of him organizing one of Trish's shows in Doha; a picture of the work Trish had made for and given him—a pencil drawing that said, "You loved me like a distant star." Obviously, I answered each and every one of his messages, even though I didn't fully understand why he was sending me them. Was it an exhibitionist urge? Do curators, aside from putting together shows at museums and galleries, feel an impulse to exhibit their own life, as if it were some extravagant art show on the Internet?

I had become the perfect voyeur, the passive spectator who lovingly accepted all I was told to look at, even if it was foolish, ugly, or boring. For the sake of being close to international art, I wasted precious hours of work paying attention to the emails Alex would send me. Furthermore, I wasted even more time racking my brain for the most ingenious of responses that would catch him by surprise. That would convince him that it was worth it to be friends with me. Seeing as I knew that he had studied classical languages in college and loved Latin poets, I would search for quotes in Latin to embed in my emails like precious stones so as to impress him with my knowledge of the ancient world. (Though really, who doesn't know how to Google a quote?) One time, I started a message with a verse from Catullus: *miser Catule, desinas ineptire*. Perversely, he would forward me the lewd messages that Trisha would send him: "I bet you fuck me up the arse before the walls are even painted Prussian blue," and the like.

I don't really know what reason I had to play witness to the failed romance between Alex and Trish. Perhaps because I'm Argentine, and for two first-world citizens who are part of the global art scene, an Argentine translator is like a maid in front of whom you don't mind showing your abhorrent side, because you don't consider her to be a full human being. In the days that followed the dinner, Alexander asked me to accompany him to each of his meetings with Trisha. I imagine it was his tactic to avoid having to have sex with her. My presence served as a symbolic chastity belt against the psychotically uncontrollable impulses of that Brit. We went to restaurants, to millionaires' houses, for strolls along avenues, to English pubs, and the traditional cafés of Buenos Aires. The situation was always more or less the same: Trisha got drunk and began calling Alex "Alejandro" (with an aspirated "j," of course, like any English speaker), saying incoherent things that semi resembled sexual advances. After a few hours, her desire would devolve into hatred, and she would insult him until the alcohol became too much to handle, and she would pass out in some armchair nearby. Then, we would revive her, help her up, and take her back to her hotel in a cab.

But a few days after the exhibit opened, on the night before both of them were to head back to the northern hemisphere, Trisha got terribly violent. We were at the house of a collector who had organized a cocktail hour. Amidst crude sculptures by young artists made out of trash bags (which blended visually with the black carpaccio trays circulating around us), Trish mustered all of her lust for Alex and funneled it into her final attempt to get him to sleep with her.

"It's our last night in Buenos Aires. You *have* to come with me," she told him, in a demanding tone. But upon realizing the curator wouldn't give in to her demands, she stood on a table and began to scream, pointing at him. "What are you?! You're just a curator. You're nothing. You're nothing. You are nothing! Just a curator—nothing! You're nothing!" She repeated those words at least twenty times.

Alex remained quiet. Then, a tray full of tall glasses with a blue drink in them passed by. Without thinking about it, Trish bent down, grabbed one, and drank it in one swift chug. The sugary alcohol seemed to give her a moment of lucidity before her consciousness collapsed again and she continued on.

"You are nothing, and I am a great artist. So if you want to talk to me, first create a work of art, and then call me!" And with those words, she got off the table, grabbed her coat, and stormed down the stairs.

Having drunk a few of the blue drinks in my attempts to emulate Trisha, I threw up three times during my cab ride home. Luckily, none were inside the car. I was caring enough to do it while we were stopped at red lights, leaning out of the open car door. It's not an interesting thing to share—the fact that I vomited after drinking four caipirinhas and two blue curacaos—for it could have happened to anybody, especially in that environment. But with that corporeal action, I felt like, once and for all, I had left behind the glamorous and pervasive world of contemporary art, which, though I was never really a part of it, I had spent months daydreaming about.

People who make a business out of art exchange their souls for money. And a work of art can't be trapped in a mansion. It must fly freely through the atmosphere and leave a trail in the air that surrounds our planet. At least this is what my teachers taught me.

Three months later, I found out that they fired Alex from the museum. Within a few days, I got an email from him, too, telling me that he'd written his first poem, and soon, he would show it to me.

Dear Johanna

I won't be able to create that work of art entailing 320 pounds of raw meat thrown against the gallery wall. Meat is just too expensive. Food has become a luxury item. I would love to do it and send you a video with the visuals for your biennial in Lima, but without financial backing, it's simply not possible. And I don't think I'll find funding in Buenos Aires unless you know of some Peruvian art collector willing to cover the expenses. Let me know if you have anyone in mind. I do have another project idea that's much simpler and equally effective, but I'm curious what you think of it. My work would involve fire. The idea is to assemble a network of people in Lima and Buenos Aires and organize a mass burning of Nike sneakers in both cities on the same day. Everyone who wants to participate just has to wear their Nike sneakers on the same day and then set them ablaze in a huge bonfire in front of the Obelisk in Buenos Aires and the Plaza de Armas in Peru. Or maybe in San Martín Plaza, since both cities have one. What do you think? I know it doesn't have the same plasticity as meat hurled against the immaculate wall of a white cube... The meat would cause an explosion of color and a disgusting, repulsive effect, which is what we both want, but burning sneakers is a much more intense work of art. No? Afterwards, we could hand out sneakers from domestic brands, to make a statement about Latin American unity and our countries' commercial solidarity. Though I don't really care to get into the conceptual implications of the work... I'm only thinking of it in visual terms: the fire melting all that synthetic rubber, the flames, the purple cloud of smoke... I don't know. Let the critics decide what it means. Anyway, hope to hear back soon.

Sergio and I

I arrived at the Recoleta Cultural Center around 4 o'clock. The performance was scheduled to start at 8 p.m. I took the H train to get there and got off at the Las Heras Station, which just opened a few months ago. For a change, when I left the station, I walked in the wrong direction for three blocks before realizing that Junín Street, where I needed to turn left, was in the other direction. It was the Starbucks that made me realize. I remembered that the store with the green logo belonged on the other side of Pueyrredón Avenue. I needed to be walking down Las Heras, as the building numbers decreased. I don't know if this lack of a sense of a direction is something you acquire in life or inherit. I'm inclined to think it's a neurological condition I was born with. I could never read maps, for example. Even if I study them for hours, the only way I've ever managed to reach an unfamiliar part of the city has been by asking others for directions. Even then, I still don't manage half the time, because I start walking and after two blocks, I get mixed up and forget all the directions. I don't know if avant-garde art has something to do with it, causing some kind of mental defect or illness or perpetually skewed vision of things. Maybe. On the other hand, I'm not convinced that what we had planned for the day was "avant-garde art," though Sergio always says that he and his friends (including me) are the only avant-garde artists in Argentina and we ought to have an audience with the president. "I WANT A FORMAL INVITATION FROM MACRI TO THE CASA ROSADA IN THE NAME OF THE ARGENTINE UNDERGROUND SCENE," he wrote on his Facebook page a few days before the show. I knew about it because, for the show, I copied a few dozen of Sergio's Facebook statuses by hand with a pencil in the last pages of a copy of *A Season in Hell* I bought especially for the event. The show was a kind of multimedia spectacle, concocted by Sergio and funded by the City government, that consisted of the following: Ulises Conti would play a few original compositions on the piano as I read fragments of Arthur Rimbaud's *A Season in Hell*. Behind us, a giant screen would project images of Portlligat (the town where Salvador Dalí lived): waves crashing against the rocks, mainly, and a kind of enormous soft-boiled egg. (In truth, I never got to see the images during the show, as my back was always to the screen.) A few moments before the end, a snow machine mounted to the ceiling would rain fake snow from over Ulises' and my heads. "That was the most beautiful part," everyone told me. In the beginning, I didn't realize that I needed to take a few steps back to end up directly below the snow machine, but Juliana signaled to me from the second row, and luckily, I managed to step back on time and feel fake snowballs soak my black crepe-paper dress. I could barely move. Sergio had assembled the dress together around my body (I had to get naked in front of all the technicians, but I didn't care) a few minutes before the show started. The whole dress was made out of black crepe paper. He tightened the top on me with clear packing tape, but he did it so tight that, at first, I could barely breathe and was worried I would choke to death. Even worse, though I didn't know about it at the time, I had a UTI and was feeling weak. Luckily, the material slowly loosened up a bit. The lower half of the piece consisted of a skirt made out of yards and yards of the same paper, black as night, which two assistants had been piecing and taping together on a massive table since 3 in the afternoon. When he had to go around me a hundred times with the packing tape, Sergio told me not to move, and for a split second, wrapped up and held tight by the tape's embrace, I felt slim and svelte. I think that was one of Sergio's talents, making everyone feel svelte, like models. A little while before, about thirty minutes before getting there, Sergio told me that I had a belly. He also said my glasses would ruin the whole visual concept of the show and I have a bad sense of fashion. After listening to me read a few of the poems during the sound test, he told me Rimbaud hadn't let himself be revealed yet. Sergio could be like that, catty and cruel, but in such a light-hearted way that it ended up sounding generous. That was one of the great mysteries of Sergio: the way the whole world loved and adored him even if he was saying the most terrible things, always drawing attention to the bad. Maybe it was because his negativity was absolute, which is something quite exclusive in today's world. And it's true, I was a little overweight. And the glasses I bought weren't the most stylish; they were cheap. And I read poorly during the rehearsal. I didn't articulate my words. No, I murmured like I was asleep, afraid of putting too much emphasis on how I read. Because emphasis is the opposite of cool, and I wanted to be cool.

Every Picture I Ever Threw Away

Throwing away pictures is odd, and I regret having done it. I don't know why I did it. Maybe it's just another part of my maladjusted behavior, as psychiatrists call it. Or maybe I only wanted to throw them away so I could feel like a heroine fighting today's world. In this day and age, when everyone else would kill to have works of art in their apartment, I throw them away. Yet this explanation, while fitting, is not true. The truth is I threw them out impulsively, an inexplicable impulse. (All impulses are inexplicable.) What's more, I had a different reason for throwing away each painting.

The first one I tossed was by an artist lover, whom I met when I was 23. His name was Ernesto. He lived on the corner of Tucumán Street and Guardia Vieja. One time, I went over to his house after a heated phone argument, and he wouldn't open the door for me even though he was the one who told me to come over. I waited, like, twenty minutes outside his door and then took a taxi home. It was 3:30 in the morning, and I was furious when I made it back to my apartment in Congreso. Forty minutes later, he claimed he had been passed out, drunk, on the bathroom floor. But that wasn't when I threw out his painting. I didn't do it out of spite. After that incident, we never saw each other again. The painting, which was quite big (about 40-by-30 inches), stayed on my living room wall for another two or three years. One day, after dropping acid (the one and only time I've tried acid in my life), some sort of identity crisis overtook me. Who am I? And who are my friends? Do I have allies or are they all frenemies? Back then, there was no Internet, and I didn't know or use the word "frenemy," but I think if that word had already been coined and popularized in Argentina, I wouldn't have had the meltdown I did, for I would have been able to work out those mixed emotions I felt toward certain people.

In any event, during that meltdown, which gave way to a crying fit where I paced around the house throwing everything that anybody ever gave me into a black garbage bag, I destroyed two paintings. One was a black painting by Carolina, my main frenemy at the time (another borderline artist like me with whom I had an almost symbiotic relationship). The other was Ernesto's. Before throwing away Ernesto's, I engaged in my own artistic intervention with it. I took out a box of pictures that I had in my closet (almost all of them were of friends) and glued them onto the painting. Then, on top of the images, I drew motion lines with a black marker and added words like "Boo!" "Ahh!" and "Bleh!" with exclamation marks. Three days later, at 3 in the morning, I took it downstairs in the elevator and left it leaning against a tree on the sidewalk. I have no idea who might have taken it. I don't know if Ernesto still shows his works today. I lit Carolina's painting on fire in the kitchen sink and then threw the ashes out through a little rectangular window overlooking

Luis Sáenz Peña Street near the corner of Hipólito Yrigoyen. The whole kitchen was painted yellow; they say yellow is the color of madness. I felt like Carolina was treating me poorly because there was a party where she went to bed with a boy I was just starting to see. Perhaps art makes fertile ground for developing frenemies or for "frenemyships" to grow on their own, like weeds in an unkempt garden.

Another painting I threw out, years later, was another huge one with a black background and spirals of something white and pink. An artist gave it to me after she asked me to help "draft" her artist statement to apply for a residency in Norway. I went one morning to her house, and we spoke a little about what she wanted to write. Truthfully, she had no idea what she was doing or why she was doing it, and being as shy as she was, getting the words out of her was like uncorking a bottle. Nevertheless, I think I managed to throw together two or three paragraphs. Months later, she told me to swing by and take a painting of my choosing. That was the payment we had agreed upon. But I was so busy and had so little time that I decided not to pick one out myself and sent my boyfriend to do it instead. He went and brought it back on his bike. When I saw it, it didn't really captivate me. Also, it was huge. I hung it up in the kitchen, where a layer of grease gradually built up on it—that grease that lingers in the air when you grill steaks. But the painting was too big to move to the living room, and it wasn't a painting I wanted or even a painting by a close friend I loved. Looking at it didn't give me the warm feeling of a friend's affection. You could say I was indifferent to the painting, and it may very well have stayed up in my kitchen for years had

I not one day gone into my boyfriend's emails and seen that he had a "thing" with the painter. It was during a few months when we were on a break, and each one of us did our own thing. I think they slept together just once. Now that he and I have reconciled and are happy again, it pains me to think about this and realize how loneliness and a lack of love can bring you to do horrific things, like deforming your body, hurting others, or throwing out works of art. After reading the email where she told my boyfriend that she had had a great time with him and her bed still smelled like him, I took the painting off the wall, placed it on the kitchen counter, and doused it in hot oil from a frying pan on the stovetop. The black acrylic melted a bit and began dripping, forming disgusting globs. None of the original image held up; the pink spirals faded as they devolved into a filthy gray. I think what the painting wanted to portray was part of the merengue covering of a quinceañera cake. Ignoring the emotionally charged pain and destruction behind my totally reprehensible gesture, you could say that the work implicitly begged for a culinary ending like that. It was born from the dissection of an ordinary, edible object like a cake, and then turned the cake into something lofty and transcendent, removed from the hustle and bustle of ordinary, mortal life. A painting is always thought of as a legacy destined for future generations. But this work died on a kitchen counter with its paint melted into an inedible mass that evoked the texture of a burnt brownie.

It's quite possible that all works of art tacitly demand their own end by way of what they show or demonstrate on a literal level.

The fourth and final work I threw away was a photograph of some leather boots cut down the middle and shot head-on. What you actually saw were four half-boots. I really did love that work, so I don't know why I gave it to Ilsa, the woman who used to come clean my house every week from 2008 to 2015. About five years ago (I think under the influence of one of those famous Japanese YouTube stars that teach you how to organize your closet), I got rid of 70 percent of my clothes and shoes. I put everything into black trash bags and asked Ilsa if she wanted them. She said yes. That same day, she had dusted the photograph of the boots and it fell off the wall. After seeing the photograph on the floor, I didn't feel like hanging it back up.

Swedenborg vs. Kant

Are you embarrassed, embarrassed of what you?
You just do too much
You need to rediscover the joy of thinking
—Peaches

Thinking.

All Paz cares about in life is thinking. And writing on her blog. Every morning, she wakes up early, and before going to her job at the mall, she makes coffee and begins writing a post.

Satellites are the saints of my religion—angels orbiting
Earth instantaneously carrying my thoughts to wherever
they are summoned.

She stops, drumming her fingers on the keyboard. She does it softly. Paz loves listening to that soundtrack of hesitation. In reality, on a blog, hesitation doesn't matter. Doubts don't matter. There's always time for redemption. Or to put it a bit less dramatically, there's always room for improvement. A blog isn't important. And even if it is, it's a kind of importance that's yet to come. "Some day, my blog will be better...

more intense... It will draw more people... It'll have thousands of readers every day... And win some prize in Germany... I've got time... I'm young yet," she says, taking her first sip of coffee.

Paz continues today's post:

In 1747, Swedenborg said that all angels were joined in a kind of all-encompassing communitas. *Every sign is manifested and exchanged between them in an unmediated way, without any errors in translation. And despite the fact that, in a well-known letter, Kant claimed Swedenborg had lost his mind, history has shown that he wasn't crazy. The Internet is a community of angels, and I love Swedenborg and hate Kant.*

Paz pauses again. The table where she's eating and writing is close to a window overlooking her garden. She's got another hour before she needs to get to work. It's winter. On the foggy glass she writes "Swedenborg" and "Kant," encircling both with a heart pierced by an arrow. The whole drawing comes undone quickly as the condensation drips and small drops of water drag larger ones with them, leaving an empty circle on the glass through which Paz can see out. During this time of year, the sun only makes a brief appearance in that part of the house for just a few hours, falling on the back wall like a triangle ruler before extending a few more inches over the edge of a flowerpot housing a light pink flower. Paz looks at the flowerpot, her laptop screen, the fern, the avocado tree, then back at her screen. She wonders whether or not she should add anything more to this post. If, for instance, it would be interesting to contrast the popular notion of "cyber-space" with the categories of space and time as formulated by Kant. She feels like space and time aren't in and of themselves categories a priori, as the German philosopher thought of them (actually, the way that her ex, Marisol, told her that Kant thought of them). She's certain that if those forms had ever existed in her spirit, they've long since been altered by her addiction to the Internet.

For example, last night she dreamt of a forest that looked like a drawing. But at the same time, she felt so comfortable and content that it felt real. When she woke up, she spent a few minutes wondering about the landscape's origin. It just seemed too familiar to be nothing more than a dreamful whim. Was it a place she had visited as a child? Maybe they were woods she once walked through, afraid, clutching her father's hands, when she was 5 years old, somewhere in the south... Finally, she realized where the vision had come from. It was a scene from Second Life, a free virtual world online where there's a place called The Paradise of Medusas—a forest of tall, marblewood trees. She loved it so much that she had gone there hundreds of times. She logged on at all times of day, talking to other people (well avatars—but they're people, too), absorbing the colors and lighting in detail. Sitting around, waiting for the action to begin. Every once in awhile, the weirdest thing would happen: Dozens of medusas would descend from the trees and have sex with each other.

After recalling her adventures in Second Life, Paz realized that new categories of space were dwelling in her spirit. She started to call Marisol to share this revelation, but changed her mind.

She stopped and went into the kitchen, where she turned on a burner to warm up her hands. Staring at the flames also helped her think.

"If space can be rebuilt by technology, then it's most probable that space doesn't truly exist. In that case, what Swedenborg proposed is more like a metaphor, a scientific truth about the nature of particles," she thought, remembering having read somewhere that an Irish physicist, named John Bell or something like that, once said that space doesn't exist and we live in a non-localized universe.

But quantum physics was something Paz would have to research another time. Maybe tomorrow, when she doesn't have to work. For now, she wants to explore why she felt so drawn to that forest that she later visited it in her dream.

"What interested me was sex with strangers. And by that, I'm referring to truly *strange* beings, like, people who are so weird that they choose to become such enigmatic and undulant beings as those medusas," she reflected.

And she was happy with that conclusion. But then she second-guessed it. As it were, she couldn't write such a long reflection on her blog, which on principle ought to be brief. Posts must be short. That was the bloggers' code, and she wasn't going to challenge it. She felt intuitively that contemporaneity favors brevity. Posts with fewer than a hundred words were the universal progressive format. Following that logic, a person must navigate cyberspace if they want to contribute to the desired change of era. A blog isn't a doctoral thesis or a novel.

It's not an object sitting on the shore of the world, to be treated as a rarity or interpreted away. Although it's fine to explain the world. That's also part of the bloggers' code. Their task is to interpret the world and the human collective. But the accumulation of goods? No way. *That* is evil. There are already too many objects on the face of the earth. Too many loose objects, opaque, autonomous things. Too much stock in factories and supermarket warehouses. Too many stray thoughts in books of poetry. And in that sense, books are no different than the shiny, acrylic toy motorcycles made in China by the millions and shipped by freight around the world. Toys are contaminating the planet. Ships are changing the makeup of the oceans. Writing is necessary, of course. Not for the sake of accumulating goods, but to connect goods with people and people with people in a new and inspiring way. Such a task could never be accomplished with the style of writing borne by as archaic an industry as publishing.

In any case, Paz had never read any of Kant's or Swedenborg's works completely. She did own the "Classics of Western Thought," a fifty-volume, green, faux-leather-bound set collecting dust on the shelf above her TV, but at that point, she hadn't ever had the time to read them (nor did she even really want to). There was something about books that turned her off. As if in some rebellious or primitive place in her nature, there was a hidden drive to remain uncontaminated by the culture of books. She came into this world under the constellation of the Internet and wanted to stay in tune with it. True, she does use philosophers' names in her blog posts, but that was merely a strategy to attract more readers. Because that was another part of the bloggers' philosophy: always boost your readership, reach more people, and expand your communication. After writing posts that were quite unpolished, she realized she got far more hits when she threw in the name of somebody well known or prestigious. That's how it occurred to her to write about Swedenborg and Kant. Well, not *just* that. She did genuinely like Swedenborg. But he was the exception. Paz didn't actually want to debate with these philosophers. She just wanted to pretend like she was debating them. She liked thinking, but she didn't want to fall into a discipline as antiquated as philosophy. Because above all else, Paz was a feminist, and she felt like philosophy had always been a field of men. Technology from the world of men who hole up in their offices to write. No, Paz wanted to democratize knowledge, make it more contemporary. That's why almost all of her ideas come from television. She listens intently to what is said on different programs and draws her own conclusions. She had always been satisfied with the ideas she came up with. What she liked most was watching music videos. All of 20th-century history was summed up in music videos. For example, watching music videos, she realized that globalization was a good thing. In turn, Marisol, a liberal arts student, had thought globalization was bad.

Thinking of Marisol, Paz remembered why she disliked Kant. One of those summer nights when, after making love, the two of them would cuddle and stargaze out the window, talking about their impressions on life, Marisol had told her that Kant had only left his hometown twice. He spent his whole life—all eighty-one years of it—indoors writing.

Swedenborg, in turn, he had a fascinating life! He had been a mathematician, a sailor, a merchant, a poet, a hydrographer, a watchmaker, and an astronomer, among many other things. His life was based on intra-activity, that is, getting involved in as many diverse contexts as possible. And the most incredible part of it all: He spoke with ghosts and angels. And in that way, he was three centuries ahead of the Internet. Okay, sure, Paz never went to college. She just worked on the window-display team at a mall. Maybe she didn't have the merit to declare such a thing at a philosophy summit at Harvard. But nobody could stop her from saying it on her blog. And she was prone to think with all possible intensity, supported only by her own blog, though she did it with the clumsiness of one whose mind is better described as a multicolor patchwork made up of vague notions and affects than a serious, organized rationalist building with sixteen delineated floors. At the end of the day, most people's minds are more like a patchwork than a building, and intensity of thought was part of that patchwork state of consciousness. Nobody could deny that.

She remembers how Marisol would say to her, "You're so naive. You don't get it. You haven't read Hegel or Marx. You're so naive." Paz would never answer, because she was afraid of Marisol. But internally she felt true enjoyment in being naive. She felt like ingenuity would take her much further in life than irony and arrogance—the only attitudes that Marisol, a philosophy major, ever had. When they went to parties, for instance, it always made her look bad. It was enough for any-body to bring up any subject for Marisol to answer with a string of terminology pulled from the university lexicon, like "consciousness of itself and for itself," "the institutional development of antagonism," or "blah blah blah." Anybody who wasn't in the same department as Marisol couldn't even begin to understand such concepts. They didn't know how to respond, so the conversations would die off with no shot of rescue. The other queer women they knew gradually stopped inviting them to get-togethers and birthdays, and one day the invitations ceased altogether. They had nothing fun left to do on Saturday nights. Marisol didn't like anything other than philosophy, and the only thing she liked doing after reading was fucking. Soon, Paz chose to end things in the name of thought: "Being with somebody as arrogant as you stifles my thinking," she said sharply.

Luckily, that dark era had ended, and now Paz again felt calm and happy. She had discovered the world of blogging, and more important, she had fallen in love again.

After thinking all of these exciting thoughts, Paz went back to the living room. But when she tried to resume her cup of coffee, she realized it had gone cold. She looked at the clock and noticed she had just twenty minutes left to finish her post. Fortunately, the bloggers' code also said to post without proofreading. Spontaneity was key to communication. Thus, before leaving, she would finish her post and feel satisfied with the message she had haphazardly offered up to the world today. She then felt that the best thing she could do was use the words and time she had left to write about thinking and love.

Since I'm with Nora, I feel like I can really think. Cause I'm in love. And women think through love.

Losing Weight

When it comes to all the kids who are skinny—too skinny, almost skeletal—that I see coming out of my son's school or coming over to spend the afternoon with him in our canvas pool, I've noticed that their mothers invariably tend to be more on the obese side. The fathers, for their part, have already surpassed that. When I see a family like that, I think, "They must not eat well." On other occasions, in my neighborhood's bargain supermarket, which has an upstairs section with bowling lanes, I see families with obese children and mothers. There are three-year-olds, four-year-olds, all of them extremely overweight eating hotdogs. My son also eats hotdogs and hamburgers sometimes. He isn't fat, but he's also not one of those kids who looks too skinny, like all the kids in his class or the ones that my aunt says are too skinny because their mother's don't make sure they finish all the food on their plate.

About three weeks ago, I went to a poet's birthday party. She and I were close in our twenties, but then we stopped hanging out. Tini was a poet, novelist, and singer who inspired me. For about two years, we hooked up from time to time. (And once, I even fucked her boyfriend, whom I now find gross, but we never realize what we're doing when we're young.) She was turning 40, and she looked quite slender. Not too skinny, like extremely slender, but rather, elegant, with an animal-print jumpsuit and some important jewel on her neck.

"You're so thin, Tini," I told her.

"It's because I gave up bleached flour," she responded. "And also because I'm happy now. I've overcome my anxiety and don't keep ice cream bars in the freezer anymore."

When I see the school moms, and I see the image of what I don't want to be (they must look at me and think the same thing, though for other reasons), I think of a shared place: obesity and lack of sexual satisfaction go hand-in-hand. I mean, everything is interconnected, and the fact that this is a school that promotes itself as "demanding" must have something to do with the lack of sexual satisfaction of the parents who send their children there. These are the things I think up as I stand at the school entrance and see people exerting great effort to look like a family—a social structure that, by definition, is imbued with the essence of dissatisfaction. Between 60 and 70 percent of the women and men who come to this institution to pick up their kids are fat.

One time, about twelve years ago, during her boyfriend Guadalupe's birthday (who also went to college with Tini and me), Tini told me the plot of a novel she was thinking of writing. To lose weight, a girl creates and sticks to a plan in which every time she feels like eating, she leaves her house and tries fucking the first man she runs into. She puts aside all classism or her standards in men (which are almost always based on an image constructed from our aspirations of social climbing), and she simply makes herself available for sex. And it works. She sleeps with the doorman, the electrician who just happened to be fixing a light in her building's stairwell, a stranger walking along Corrientes Street. And she loses weight. Instead of eating six croissants, she looks for somebody to have sex with. She's replaced sugar for orgasms.

When I heard the words coming out of Tini's mouth about food in the middle of her birthday, I didn't think about quelling my anxiety or really anything about anxiety at all. What I felt, rather, was that losing weight was a way to remove a bit of myself from this world. "The total mass that my being occupies on this planet will be less if I lose weight. There will be more free space for others, for air, or even just for the sun," I thought. I felt like no longer eating the things I love most—bread, pastries, chocolate, cookies, and cake— could be a path of spiritual learning, like a means of preparation for aesthetic sovereignty. Not being dependent on food or any other substance to be happy. I felt like only a free spirit could achieve this... or an ascetic spirit.

Are asceticism and freedom one and the same?

Perhaps they're close; perhaps they're opposites... In any event, I just recently crossed the threshold of my forties, that period of life we think of when we're young as the beginning of the end of it all, but then when it actually comes it doesn't feel like that whatsoever.

Forty is like a two-story house with carpeting and lots of natural light. Or like a lavender-purple silk slip on a king-sized bed with a satin comforter.

I remember when I was 25, I thought I wanted to be 40 and dress just like Cher: in tight leather miniskirts or really anything black, shiny, and ripped up. I also pictured myself wearing velvet breeches.

At 41, it makes me happy to think that I may recover purity. I love the idea of eating healthy, smooth, illuminating foods. I love that idea, even if I know it's just an idea. Or maybe I love it precisely because it's a concept above all. And concepts precede reality.

* * *

It's been three months since Tini's birthday, the day I decided to stop eating flour and sugar in an act that was a mix of envy and admiration. I don't know if I've really lost weight, because it was winter then, and on the drug store scale with clothes and heavy shoes, you obviously always weigh more. I've certainly gained a few pounds, but now that I'm naked it looks like I weigh the same as before or maybe lost weight... I know that for days or weeks on end, I managed to avoid foods with flour or sugar, but then I ate chocolate and croissants. Croissants were the hardest thing for me to give up because they're one of my favorites. I also ate pizza one time when there was nothing else to eat. Or pizza rolls and cake at some birthday party where I went to pick up my son a few minutes before it ended... The idea of achieving aesthetic and spiritual sovereignty through food wasn't as easy as I thought it would be. And what if, instead of eating well, I commit to writing better? I know that at 41, I don't really have any other option. I must write well, I must write well, I must write well. If I want to be anybody in this life. Or at the very least, I must try.

I'm going to call Tini to tell her that we must write well.

Flourishing Peach II

For Fernanda Laguna

I'm one of those people who only ever think about their love life, and I'm married. I'd like to think that my husband is the kindest man in the world, but my husband is the most evil man in the world. At least that's the reputation he has in the tiny world we live in—the young poetry scene of Viña del Mar. (He's a critic and I'm a cover illustrator.)

My husband is a handsome man. He's 6 feet tall, and you could describe his beauty as almost feline. His eyes are slanted. His body, slender but strong. He dresses like a teenager and smokes expensive Cuban cigars, which further accentuate his natural elegance. I love him, endlessly, and nothing could ever make me want to leave him. Unfortunately, his biggest enemy on the literary scene is my best friend, a romance novelist by the name of Flourishing Peach. Their feud creates a lot of marital problems for us. All-day fights that end with doors being slammed, and one time, I even threw his laptop out the window and it crashed in the middle of the street. (We live on the seventh floor.)

Flourishing Peach isn't my friend's real name, you see. It's the pen name she chose to start writing novels about surfer girls and the like. Almost all of her novels are about girls with strange jobs. The latest, for example, was called *Roaring Lion*, and it's the story of a caretaker at the Berlin zoo who paints portraits of the animals in her free time. I don't want to reveal anyone's identity, so I'll make up names for them. Flourishing Peach will be Lily. Lily has had extraordinary success with circles of young readers in Viña del Mar, and her success is spreading through all of Chile, and other countries too. Given how unconventional they are (take, for instance, *Packed Cells*, about a hundred female tattoo artists in jail for running unregulated tattoo parlors in Concón and Reñaca), her novels are well written, in the sense that you can read them easily and enjoy yourself. Or at the very least, they've got something about them, how can I explain it... Like a drug, something that makes them impossible to put down. Everyone says they're addictive, and thanks to her commercial success, Flourishing Peach was able to move out of her tiny, dark apartment full of cockroaches to one of those newly built residential towers with an ocean view and entrances lined by a sea of gardens and climbing plants brought in from Brazil.

What is it that bothers my husband so much? I don't know. He's never explained it to me. At this very moment, he's working on a long article analyzing all of the technical failures in *Yellow, Phosphorescent Hearts*, my friend's latest success. As I make dinner, I secretly spy on him. At the end of the day, I love my husband, but Lily has been my friend since I was 13. Sometimes I visit her and we take a break under the refreshing ocean breeze. We sit on her patio set and quietly watch the sky. She'll lend me a spare pair of sunglasses so my eyes don't get hurt, a pair she bought on one of the trips she's taken. And like that, behind dark lenses, we sit quietly, passing the time.

Lily's husband is younger than she is. He works as a serviceman at a gas station and writes journals that he publishes in hole-punched photocopies that he binds with threads of yellow string. He gives them out to Argentine tourists at the beach, because no bookstore in Viña del Mar wants to sell them on consignment. In Viña del Mar, there are no indie bookstores or anything like that.

Lily isn't worried about my husband's critiques. Honestly, she doesn't understand them, because they're too complicated, written in an almost scientific register. She's "decided not to implicate herself in Byzantine debates," to use her own words. "Every day, I feel more secure," she says sometimes, and it sounds like it's lifted right out of a self-help book. But the forcefulness with which she says it, the conviction… those come from the world of artistic inspiration, of that I'm sure. Lily is definitely an inspired woman. I admire her. She gets up at 8 a.m. each day, runs two miles along the coast, then goes home and writes, writes, and writes. She hardly eats until nighttime, and even then, she just has something light. (She's very thin.) She doesn't smoke or drink either. Her husband usually eats lunch and dinner at the gas station because he works a full shift. He says that he loves the smell of gasoline. But the same smell nauseates Lily. It makes her kind of light-headed, so she never goes to visit him. "My drugs, my vacations, and my passion are my novels," she always says. She's always saying things like that. Which, I must confess, I find annoying sometimes. I'd honestly rather go to her house and sit in silence. In her living room, there are bookshelves from wall to wall with all the classics, including Cervantes, the Bible, Dante, and so on, and another shelf with all the Chilean classics, such as Neruda, Carrasco, and Mistral. But most of her personal library is just her own work, every edition of every book, including translations. She's been translated into Japanese, Chinese, and German. In China, she's a best seller on the same level as Harry Potter; pirated copies of her books are sold on the streets of Shanghai. It doesn't bother her though. In fact, she loves it, even if she's losing money.

My husband is the most beautiful man in Chile. One day, we were walking along Paseo Ahumada, hand in hand, enjoying spring just like back when we first met, and we ran into Lily.

"Hi."

"Hi."

Followed by an icy silence.

"What were you guys up to around here?"

"Nothing much. It's our day off, so we were just walking around. How about you?"

"Oh, nothing. I'm on my way home from a cocktail party. It was the debut of my latest novel. I was signing books, kids were handing me letters, the mayor gave me a medal, blah blah blah."

My husband (now I'll tell you the name I made up for him: Louis) grabbed my waist and interrupted her, saying, "We have to go. It's getting late for us."

She answered, "Hang on, I actually wanted to ask you two out for a drink. Please?"

Louis didn't know what to say. I didn't know what to say. What would come of this? "Sure," we said at the same time.

We followed Flourishing Peach to one of those small café-bars with plastic tables on the sidewalk. It was on a short, narrow street, and across from the bar, there was a flower shop. It was a beautiful spot... the smell of jasmine mixed with coffee, two hummingbirds hovered over white roses.

"Well," she said, as soon as we sat down. "I'd like for you to tell me, Louis, exactly what it is that you don't like about my novels."

Louis stayed silent, muttering something incomprehensible that sounded like it was an answer, but his nerves got the best of him. "You can read it in my articles," he said, after several seconds of silence. "There's a reason I write them after all."

"Yes," she said. "I know that you write them for a reason. I just wanted to hear it from your own lips. For you to tell me in person, face to face."

"Well okay," he stared straight into her eyes, with that feline look I mentioned earlier. "I consider your writing to be vain, self-indulgent, obscene, and neglectful of the most important thing: Form. Form—the only truth in Literature. Form—the only space for communal redemption, detachment from the bourgeois ego, and any proximity to the impersonal. Form—the only operation by which aesthetics become political. Your novels don't respect Form. Furthermore, you write for the sake of writing, you're irresponsible, blah blah blah."

After hearing this, Flourishing Peach stood up and ran off with her hands over her face. I felt like those words had been a dagger stabbing her in the heart. I stayed there with Louis and gripped his arm. Flourishing Peach disappeared off into the streets of Viña del Mar.

Unlimited Budget

The long road of it all
is an echo
a sound like an image
expanding, frames growing
one after another in ascending
or descending order, all
of us a rising, falling
thought, an explosion
of emptiness soon forgotten
—Robert Creeley

I hear a bell chime twice: it's 2 o'clock. I've got six more hours to sleep. I didn't sleep at all last night. This is my second night of insomnia. My husband breathes heavily, turns over, moves his hand in a strange way. I try to read each movement he makes in our bed as if it spelled out a letter. He's writing something in the wrinkles of our sheets, perhaps with an unusual font, like the ones that produce hallucinatory effects on readers. But it's too dark to read anything. Then, I imagine I'm blind and know how to read Braille, that I'm deciphering his writing on our bed by feel. The animalistic hissing of each breath he lets out is also writing something in the warm hotel air. As if the characters, sounds, and letters were hanging from a viscous material made out of air and heat. Suddenly, he makes an abrupt movement. What word is he trying to write? Perhaps it isn't a word at all, but rather a lone, meaningless syllable from a violent, guttural poem, one made only of sounds. There are poets who write like that. Today I heard one read: a Belgian, over six feet tall and bearded, who made ridiculous jokes during lunch, which he topped off with a friendly, stupid grimace. He let out those sounds while standing in the middle of the stage, taking long pauses. Then, an Argentine read the Spanish version of the poem, but the translation was identical to the original, other than the accent. It was perfect: a universal poem intelligible to all. Being someone who writes things overloaded with meaning, I felt embarrassed about the focus of my own poetics. Always trying to say something, always trying to move my readers with my most intimate experiences. I felt like my writing was old-fashioned and outdated, like I was still so far from mounting the horse of contemporaneity, getting on board the dazzling train of empty space, the vehicle of the present. Perhaps my insomnia is a result of my doubts or anxiety. It's paralyzing, but I'm also just excited that I was even invited to this festival. Because I'm a strange body in this environment. On the way here, I thought maybe they had made some sort of mistake, that the organizers had invited me in error. If I always feel like what I write about doesn't matter to anybody, that my writing is bad, that my style is bad, that it's full of errors in syntax and grammar, that it's a waste of energy that will never move anybody other than me and my own ghosts (even though I secretly hold out hope that it will affect the ghosts of others, too), then what am I meant to do in this space where everything is about showing off how well I write? About demonstrating that I've discovered a tool so impersonal that others can also make use of it? Deep down, that's what poetry is. Or at least that's what it should be... I'm petrified of not knowing if I'll ever achieve that.

The church bell chimes three more times. It must be 3. Was I awake or asleep this past hour? The wondrous thing about insomnia is that time starts to bend. I saw things—I'm sure of that. Though I'm not sure if they came from a dream or if they're in the space that I'm occupying. Squinting, swinging lines. Spread-out, disconnected lines made of the interactions of shadows and objects. The physical things that are present (or at least they were when we arrived): a bed; a window; a TV; a reproduction of Monet hanging on the wall with a dull, glass frame; a mirror faintly lit up by a Tiffany lamp. How is it that these objects—precise and clear during the day—have become nothing but fading lines, outlines that cross each other like woven wicker, making me dizzy, uncomfortable, confused? Two nights without sleep, almost forty hours awake. It's as if the hotel room has become a gigantic work of op art that wants to violently penetrate my mind and tell me that, in reality, there is nothing to see, that sight is a useless sense, that the eye has nothing to capture in this world. I know that it's 2009—I'm still conscious of the calendar—but I feel like I'm in one of those liquid light shows they did on either side of the Atlantic in the mid-1970s from secret locations. I don't know if they had them in Latin America, too. Maybe time and space have been altered. Maybe there was a nuclear attack somewhere on the planet, and my hotel room has been tossed into a psychedelic era, like that Philip K. Dick story where some soldiers from the new temporal order find a family floating in the past and jump at the opportunity to steal all the food they have in their fridge.

Four bells chime. My husband set an alarm for 8 a.m. so we could eat breakfast together. I've only got four hours left. Slowly, I lose all hope of sleeping. Without the perspective of a rested mind, the prospect of any concept for a project grows weaker. I don't know if I'll be able to finish editing the poems I had planned on reading. I don't know if I'll be able to take in the air needed to let out the syllables making up the words written on the sheets of paper I printed before leaving. I think about my insecurities. I wonder if the other poets also share my fears. If they're sleeping calmly or if they, too, are tossing and turning like I am. I imagine conversations with them. Am I imagining them or am I really having them? Is it telepathy or a dream? I hear the bell chime five times, and I still have yet to fall asleep...

"I don't want to read sitting all stiff in front of a microphone with a spotlight glaring in my eyes," says a Peruvian poet as she grips her book tightly against her chest. It's a black book with an illustration of a snake with silver scales. "I'd rather set the chairs up in a circle so we can confess our fears to one another."

And someone with an unrecognizable, heavy voice answers, "How many of the people here feel confident about what they're doing and how many of us are afraid of rejection?"

"Yes, yes," adds a German poet in ripped-up jeans. "We should set the chairs up in a circle and then each read just one poem—the best one we have. Audiences have a limited capacity to listen. The crowd might be more interested in our fears than our writing. What we need is an unlimited budget, but not in an economic sense. Actually, yes, but in an economy of listening, not money. I repeat, the capacity to listen is limited; the festival organizers haven't taken this fact into consideration."

And stuttering, a Guatemalan poet who writes about indigenous peoples adds, "Perhaps we ought to expand our resources... What I mean is increase the capacity to listen, give the audience an infinite willingness to listen... But I can't think of how to do it... If we managed to do it, there wouldn't be any egos or hierarchies. What are aesthetic battles if not battles for the short-lived attention of your fellow humans? If such shortages didn't exist, then war wouldn't either. Each poet could have all of humanity at their disposition listening to and clapping for them."

Then somebody says, "Poetry made by robots." And a chorus of applauses goes off like a deafening waterfall descending over my bed and my body.

"Poetry festivals with chairs set up in circles where we read poetry made by robots. That's what we all want. That's the conclusion we've reached," I tell myself, whispering, and I move around a bit in bed, like a minor convulsion, while out there, in the church three blocks from our hotel, the bell chimes seven times.

It obviously doesn't make sense to try to go sleep anymore. I'll get up and get dressed, put on my makeup, and wait for my husband to wake up so we can go down to the hotel restaurant. I'm no longer afraid; now I know that all poets are just like me, that they want exactly what I want: to be replaced by robots, to be rescued from fear.

It's exciting to know that from now on, poetry will be perfect and never again will I have to write.

Jeans

With sequined back pockets. That's what the jeans I want look like. Hand-sewn sequins distributed on each pocket in a seemingly completely random way that, in fact, had to be intentional because its effect is enchanting and magical. Small sparkles dispersed over the midnight blue backdrop of the dark denim fresh from the factory, still covered in indigo dye. Sequins like fat, round fireflies buzzing over a marsh or like that glow of the waves in this part of the world where she's come.

"Ostende," she mumbles, lying in bed without opening the door. Her sneakers, mud-stained from the storm, have already left a stain on the emerald green duvet. "Ostende, Ostende," she says, continuing on like that indefinitely for what could have been a few seconds or several minutes. With each repetition, she draws out the "O" a little more, such that by the time her mother opens the door, she is immersed in a kind of mantra: "Oooooooooostende." She mumbles with her eyes closed. Her mother sits down on the adjoining bed in silence, so as not to disturb her. (They've been given a medium-sized double, but the beds are tiny and only separated by a nightstand.)

It is in no way typical that a translators conference should happen in a beachside resort in early summer, but seeing as the invitation was all-inclusive and they usually never have enough money to go on vacation, they decided to come.

The mom and the daughter have always lived together. Lila got divorced quite young, and Flora never got married. Both of them work in the same field, and they each work at either extreme of their house. However, they always come together for lunch and dinner.

"Ooostende, Oooooooooostende," Flora continues. Listening to her, her mom thinks that, in reality, Ostende could just be a strange name, dry and grave, its gravity marked by the "O," an "O" that weighs so much at the start of the word, inevitably drawn-out for lack of surrounding vowels. Compared, for instance, to the names of the neighboring resorts—Pinamar, Miramar, or Cariló—Ostende wins in terms of presence, but loses in terms of brilliance. Pinamar suggests the beauty of trees, summer, nature. Ostende, in turn: just sand and a void.

When Flora opens her eyes, it takes a few seconds for her to register that her mother is also lying down on the next bed over. She's on her side with her elbow supporting her head watching Flora.

"What do you think of the hotel?" her mom asks.

"It checks out," Flora answers, vaguely. But she isn't very interested in the hotel or the conference or (while she does love her line of work) debating technical, stylistic, or ethical aspects of translation. Her mind is equally unoccupied by concepts related to the beauty of the surrounding nature (open beaches and deserts), the hotel's architecture (the originality and perfection of which everyone mentions), or the delicacies promised by the menu distributed by the organizers. Today, all Flora can think of is clothes. She remembers the dark blue jeans with sequins that she spotted when the van they took here drove through a nearby resort town for a few minutes. The driver needed to buy something in a store downtown and stopped the van in front of a boutique shop. Flora, who had been sleeping with her head resting on her arm, opened her eyes. Looking through the window to see where they were, she saw the jeans hanging in the shop window. The shine of the sequins was bright enough to blind her.

Now, lying in bed, she realizes it would be impossible to communicate the joy she felt upon seeing those jeans to her mother, and even more so to tell her that she would love to somehow buy them.

Lila got out of bed and started to walk toward the bathroom. Flora watched her from behind. She was wearing a skirt and a shirt, both loose and a nondescript color. She had always refused to dye her hair, so at 64, it was completely white. "White like the sequins," thought Flora.

"The dinner where we meet all the other translators starts soon," said Lila. "I'll have a shower."

Flora didn't answer. She sat up in bed, crouched over, and she looked out the window. The rain had stopped, and now rough winds were blowing up large waves of sand.

"Did you know that, for a few years in the 1930s, this hotel was completely covered by sand?" she asked, but her mom had already gone into the bathroom and started running the water for her shower. (Flora had just read this fact in a promotional pamphlet the hotel kept on the nightstand.)

She could hear the sound of the water starting to run in the bathroom. The steam of a warm vapor came through the gap between the door and the floor. Flora closed her eyes again and imagined elegant people dressed in all white running through shifting dunes.

* * *

Following dinner, the translators all stayed in the gallery watching the sandstorm. Every so often, somebody murmured an interjection in some language or other, and everybody smiled.

"Sandsturm," said the German translator.

"Sandstorm," added the English translator.

"Tormenta de areia," added the Portuguese one.

Flora and Lila merely offered their most courteous smiles, but did not speak with anyone. They weren't very social. They had never been the type to see so many people. They didn't like gatherings or parties, and they spoke only once or twice a year with the little close family that they had. They generally spent all day translating—the only way to survive. Unless done as a full-time activity, working as a translator didn't pay enough. On the other hand, it was strange that neither of them had become a writer, given how much they both loved to read. They were both German translators. They translated poets, essayists, and novelists. Some good and some bad. Some fun and others tedious. But neither of them had ever taken the initiative to write something of her own. They found it shameless. Or maybe pointless. "Why add yet another letter to this world?" Lila had told her daughter, when, at 17 years old, the latter came home saying she wanted to get her degree in literature. Flora later repeated the same question at the few dances she attended during her college years. She studied German literary translation, and as soon as she graduated, she began to share her mother's jobs with her. They translated whole books as a pair, and whenever one finished a chapter, the other proofed it. At night, after a light dinner, they watched Deutsche Welle, the German channel, so as not to lose touch with the musicality of the language. They never considered visiting Europe. In fact, they hadn't ever left Argentina. But they spoke almost perfect German, and their lives were calm.

While the other conference participants spoke over each other about matters unrelated to books or languages, Flora found herself thinking about those jeans again. She had a friend who was a rock singer who wore jeans like them. They had gone to high school together, and now the friend traveled all over Latin America promoting her music. Sometimes she would call up Flora and ask to meet up in a coffee shop. They would see each other at one of the endless cafés in Recoleta, and Flora would patiently listen to all her rock star friend's adventures with record producers and TV show hosts. Her other school friend was a gallery owner, and she had been earning a lot of money lately. Flora barely had enough to get by. She and her mom shared every job, and after paying all the household bills, they divided the earnings in half. Flora's rock star friend didn't care much about Flora's life, but her gallery owner friend did. Sometimes, when they spoke on the phone, she would suggest that Flora move out on her own and leave her mom behind, because otherwise, she'd never meet a man this way. But every time, Flora would avoid responding and change the subject as quickly as she could.

That night, Flora fell into a deep sleep. Her mother stayed up late reading Robert Brinkmann and trying to translate a few lines in her head. Flora had a dream that the government wasn't allowing residents of Buenos Aires to leave the city. They installed police units at the borders separating the city from the rest of the country to prevent anybody from crossing. It was an arbitrary measure for which the president offered no explanation. Not only could nobody leave, but nobody could enter either, and all commercial activity was frozen. Quickly, consumer goods started to run out, and people began realizing they would die soon. So they began looting upscale retail stores and holding weeks-long parties in movie complexes gobbling up the last of the chocolate bars stored behind the counter.

After breakfast the following day, the owner of the hotel offered a mini tour of the building. Flora joined the tour group with enthusiasm, although her enthusiasm went unnoticed by the others. She was constantly engrossed, with her gaze always elsewhere. It was an early-20th-century French building constructed by the owner's Belgian ancestors. Just a few years after being built, the sandstorms completely covered it, and the Belgians went back to their home country. For six years, the hotel remained buried, until the family decided to have it excavated from the sand and reopened. There were two dining rooms with bright tile flooring and heavy antique wooden tables. Flora thought the layout felt like a maze, though she couldn't tell if that was reality or merely a projection of her mind. Maybe the vertigo she felt walking around with all those strangers had caused her to imagine fictional architecture. In one of the galleries, there was a whale skeleton assembled near some planters with chrysanthemums. The owner told a complicated backstory about how the bones got there, but Flora got lost thinking about those jeans again and didn't pay attention. The sandstorm and the whale skeleton were related in some way. It seemed like everything in that hotel had something to do with sand.

They reached the fourth and final floor. The owner warned everyone that the next stop on their tour, the lookout tower, wasn't for those with vertigo. You had to climb a steep and narrow stairwell in near total disrepair in order to get there. Some of the older women wearing uncomfortable shoes opted not to go up, as did some of the men with a few extra pounds to shed, who each claimed to have asthma or a bad heart. Flora wouldn't let herself miss out on visiting that mysterious place. They climbed the stairs in a single-file line as the owner explained that it was the only part of the hotel that hadn't been renovated. Upon reaching the top, a yellow yet cold light surrounded them, leaving them all speechless. For several minutes, the only sound was the creaking of old wood. The lookout tower was a hexagonal room with windows overlooking the ocean on all sides. The windows were dirty and streaky, making the beach look like a faded sticker.

Then, they announced a morning trip to the nearby spa followed by an afternoon roundtable on comparative literature. Flora felt like this was a good opportunity to go try on—and eventually buy—those jeans, though she had no idea how much they cost. She went to her room to grab her sunglasses and wallet, and she saw her mother there lying down reading.

"A van is picking us up to go to Pinamar. Do you want to go?" she asked.

"No. I'd rather stay here and take a stroll along the beach." She then added that she preferred nature to consumerism, which prompted Flora to ask her mom whether or not she considered Flora's desire to buy the jeans materialistic. It hadn't occurred to Flora that her mother's critique might have been based on that. If she had been hesitant to share her interest with her mother, it was because her mom didn't have the sense to appreciate the beauty of clothes, not because of a moral judgment hidden behind her mother's rejection. Flora recalled how, as a child, she hated her mother's clothes. She felt like her mom always wore the exact same thing: a figure-less knee-length dress (she didn't have even a single pleated dress) and a beige short-sleeve shirt. Everything was always beige. She didn't know where her mother bought her clothes. In fact, she never saw her mother come home with the shopping bags other women sometimes tote by the handful. As they walked around downtown, Flora's mother would pass by store windows without expressing the least of interest, as if they had sacks of potatoes or rows of nude mannequins inspired by a surrealist work.

When Lila turned around, Flora grabbed her wallet from the nightstand drawer quickly. She gripped it closely against her leg (as though her firm grip had the power to multiply her money) and left the room without another word.

Outside, the wind had stopped. While the tree leaves were dirty with sand, the sun gave everything a summery vibe. (Vacation season would start in just a few days.)

Flora didn't need to open her wallet and count how much money she had. She knew perfectly well how much there was, because Flora always knew how much money she had left until her next paycheck and exactly how much she had to spend on insignificant things like a cup of coffee or a movie ticket—the small mundane luxuries she had to budget for. Her wallet held exactly 83 pesos—enough to last her through the end of the translators conference. Of course, they didn't *need* to spend anything because the conference was all paid for, but Flora also knew that even if she saved them all, her 83 pesos would never be enough for those jeans. Jeans like that would obviously cost double or even triple that. And the high price is part of the magic of owning something like that. It wouldn't be the same if the jeans were cheap and easy to acquire, Flora thought, though she was embarrassed to have thought that. It felt like a dirty thought to her, in sharp contrast to the top quality and elegance of the jeans. Without a doubt, the best thing wasn't thought, but action. Action, like when she translated. That's why, in a way, translation was better than literature, where one must make hundreds of decisions every second. In turn, translation involved making very few decisions, and the choices are from a finite list of elements.

Taking action, moving forward, desiring, owning. Owning the jeans was a desire. Logic shouldn't play a role in desire. Everybody said so. If you let logic interfere with your desires, if you stop "following your heart," life becomes dull. Flora had read this in a thousand different places and heard it on thousands of TV shows. She was sure it was true.

The van stopped, and the driver said they would meet back up at the van in the same spot in two-and-a-half hours. The streets of Pinamar were empty, but most of the businesses were open. The employees were straightening up, taking out boxes, cleaning with large feather dusters, organizing window displays. The window display with the jeans seemed to be the only one that was ready. For a moment, Flora daydreamed it like a scene out of an opera or a postmodern art installation in some remote, wealthy country. The saleswoman—the guardian of this treasure—was flipping through a magazine indifferently.

Flora walked in and stopped in front of a clothing rack with shirts. This season, polka dots of all sizes and sailor stripes—red, white, and blue—were in. Then, she looked at each of the cotton dresses, which felt soft, like flower petals, in her hands, she thought. Finally, she walked over to the jeans. She didn't even stop to look at the tag. She had already dismissed the idea that she could afford them on the van. Her moves were simple and not at all professional. It was the first time she was doing something like this. Before going for it, she took a deep breath and thought, "Everyone accomplishes their dreams. Mine is to steal. To steal something for myself. Something shiny and sequined. I'm 41 years old. I'm a translator. My mother is a translator, too. I have no father or husband. Never will we, not my mother nor I, earn enough to buy a pair of jeans like this. In the years of life I have left, there won't be a miracle that changes the laws of distribution of wealth. I'm young yet. I have quite a few years left to wear a pair of jeans like this. And if some sufficiently strong revolutionary uprising coalesces to try and take power, it won't work. The market rules that dictate our existence are set in stone in the system's structure and unchangeable." And as she thought this, she wondered where she had gotten ideas like this from. She wasn't usually interested in politics and had never studied economics. And in that instant, without thinking too much, she quickly took the jeans off the hanger, slipped them into her bag, and left the shop running.

Flora didn't catch whether or not the saleswoman had noticed her theft, but her departure was so obvious that the saleswoman must certainly be calling the police already. She ran as fast as she could down the main street, leapt over the boardwalk curb like an athlete, and reached the empty beach. She had done it! She had done it! She didn't even know if the jeans were her size, but it didn't matter. The jeans were hers! If they were too small, she would lose weight so she could wear them; if they were too big, she would gain a few pounds.

Ostende was a little over four miles away, and with the beach deserted, Flora felt her heart swell with joy and liberation.

By the time she reached the hotel, it was almost 3 p.m. They had already cleared the table after lunch, and they were starting to set the dining room back up to use as a conference room. The beautiful cream linen tablecloths had disappeared, and two workers rolled a large chalkboard into the back of the room. Flora thought about going to her room, but worried that her mother would notice something about her was off and then ask too many questions, causing her to confess. Also, she wanted to try on the jeans. That was all she really wanted. She sat in the lobby for a moment, looking in either direction, as if she were keeping an eye out for anybody's arrival. When her eyes caught a glimpse of the staircase to her left, she remembered that it led up to the lookout tower. She climbed, anxious but still sly, clutching the handles of her bag. Once there, she took out the jeans and spread them on the dusty floor. At that hour, the yellow light was strong, transforming the lookout into a warm place. Flora thought about those attics packed with boxes of forgotten things, the kind that showed up all the time in the children's stories she had to translate. But here, there was nothing. Just a strange light and creaking wood. She took off her shoes, the shorts she was wearing, her shirt, her bra, everything except her underwear, and she put on the jeans. She felt like she ought to try them on like that, completely nude. It was a kind of new ritual in her life. She felt like they fit perfectly, though there was no mirror in the room to confirm that. She remembered the small pocket mirror in her purse, and her hopes soared. She took it out and stretched her arm as far up as she could, tilting her hand a little so she could see the jeans. She could only see parts of her naked body and the denim that was covering her legs and hips. She spent several minutes staring at herself, moving the mirror around to catch glimpses from various angles. A slight breeze made the glass windows creek, and Flora got startled. She took the jeans off in a rush and put the clothes she had been wearing before back on (those shorts and that floral shirt). When she looked through the window, jeans in hand, she saw a police car driving slowly down the main road. The hotel's lookout tower offered a panoramic view of the whole town. Flora got paranoid and decided it would be best to hide the jeans. If the police came for her, it would be hard for them to reach the lookout tower. And if they somehow made it up there and found the jeans, she could always blame someone else. In any event, to avoid that final possible scenario, Flora thought it would be best to hide the jeans. She lifted up one of the floorboards and carefully placed the folded jeans beneath it. Of course, she could always wash them later. But dirt and all, the jeans were still lovely.

When she went down, the round table had already started. There was just one empty seat left, next to her mother. Flora sat there. She listened to the endless presentations as they went on for hours, and then a few minutes before the final debate ended (there were debates after every presentation), she stood up and started to head for her room. Her mother followed.

"Aren't you going to eat dinner?" Lila asked. When she opened the door, she saw her daughter had gotten into bed fully dressed and already had her eyes closed.

Flora didn't answer. Lila decided not to push and went back to the dining room instead.

* * *

That same night, Flora and her mother—and all the other hotel guests, as well—woke up around 4 a.m., frightened by an alarm whose sound seemed to come from speakers embedded in the walls. Flora had fallen asleep fully dressed, so she didn't have to waste any time scrambling for something to put on, while her mother, in turn, still sleepy and disoriented, stumbled in the dark trying to find her suitcase to grab a coat. Once she found one, she told Flora to follow her, and they both ran down the hallway toward the main exit. In front of the hotel, most of their colleagues—the majority in pajamas—huddled up to stay warm. By that hour, the temperature had dropped noticeably.

A few minutes went by before Flora and her mother really understood what was going on. There had been a fire; somebody else pointed it out for them.

"Up there, in the lookout tower," said a bald hotel employee, whose lips were starting to go blue. Flora turned her neck up and saw the flames coming from the windows. She remembered the cold, yellow light that had always ruled that space, how it contrasted with the force of that fire.

She thought about the jeans.

For a minute, she wondered if she had been the one who started the fire: "Perhaps, sleepwalking, I climbed to the lookout tower and started a fire." The visual effect of the flames was strong enough to make you seasick. The smoke billowing forth from the fire finally reached them, and people were beginning to cough. Flora didn't feel well, and she walked a few feet toward the beach, her mother in tow.

"Are you alright?" she asked.

"Yeah, I just need to lie down for a few minutes."

Flora moved her hair and lay down, face up on the ground. Before closing her eyes, she looked at the stars. They reminded her of the hand-sewn sequins on her pair of jeans.

Every Bag I've Ever Owned

It's been about a year since I distanced myself from all my girlfriends. Well, to be so honest, I didn't have so many of them. Just two: Carolina and Mariana. I'm not sure what happened. We used to see each other every two to three weeks. We would take our kids to parks or meet up at somebody's house to drink and chat the night away. Art, people, literature. But at some point, our messages grew fewer and farther between. One friend started seeing a guy with a young daughter, and she started to always claim that she was exhausted or didn't have any free time. The other one started fighting with her husband and has been spending her Saturdays running around the city looking for an apartment to rent and move into. Months have gone by, and we haven't seen each other. First, I was offended. Then, Mariana was offended. And finally, Carolina stopped speaking to both of us. So then I stopped speaking to either of them, too.

After awhile, I got used to life without them. It's a mystery how girlfriends disappear. I spent months remembering them all the time until I got tired of thinking about them, too, and decided to put my mind to other things. Like every bag I've ever owned.

The first purse I ever remember having was a completely round plastic blue one with a cartoon character on it. I think underneath the character it said VIA VAI, and I was convinced my grandmother had brought it from Italy, though it's more likely she had just bought it somewhere back home in the provinces, in San Juan. When I was a child, my maternal grandmother was the only person in my family who had gone to Europe (and other exotic places like Japan and India, too), because she was rich. My grandfather had a red Mercedes Benz, and my grandmother had countless things she had bought in other countries. I don't know if I asked for that purse or if she gave it to me as a Christmas gift without me having expressed any desire for one. I know I had seen it in her house before and loved it. And I know that later, it was mine. I started to use it in the summers. Sometimes to go to the gym or the pool, though it was too small for a towel and flip-flops. It was completely round, a strange shape for a purse. Navy blue with an adjustable white strap. To be honest, I'm not sure if at some point I was overusing it. It's not like eleven-year-olds get a lot of opportunities to use a purse, especially since they're in school all day. What I remember is having seen it in the closet and thinking it was something quite exclusive and valuable because it was made in another country. Even though it was plastic, plastic wasn't as under-valued compared to leather back then as it is now. Or maybe it was, just not for an eleven-year-old.

After that I have a lot of lapses in memory about whether or not I had a purse at different times. There's a photograph of me with my sister at the Buenos Aires City Zoo wearing

Bordeaux-and-gray baggy Scottish pants with a blue leather over-the-shoulder clutch. My sister, two years younger than me, is dressed identical to me and has the same clutch, but in red. It's obviously a clutch for young girls just imitating a grown woman's purse. This was one was real leather, I think. The strap was a gold chain. It was really beautiful, but a bit formal.

Well, maybe it has something to do with the fact that in my time, pink wasn't as popular for girls. I think I was eleven.

Then came the backpack era. The ones we all had in grade school. At first, my mother picked them out for us, and then we got to pick out our own. I remember when I was nine I chose a brown bag with red and orange stripes. It wasn't a backpack like the ones all my classmates used; it was an uncomfortable messenger bag. And brown was clearly a masculine color. When I was growing up, Argentine manufacturing was precarious and fledgling. We didn't have backpacks with wheels. And the backpack itself was already an improvement, because the most common thing was to have these briefcase-like bags, leather cases whose whole weight was carried by a single handle. In the '70s (which is when I started school), we had the briefcases. But by the mid-'80s, backpacks were around. My favorite backpack, the one I loved the most, was the one I got when I was thirteen and starting high school. It was a light fuchsia or bubble-gum pink color, and was made of rubberized canvas that made it look puffy or like it was inflated by a gust of wind. It said "Tomato" in a vinyl box on the front alongside a rough drawing of a tomato painted purple.

I never saw that brand of backpack or bag in my life again. Maybe they stopped using that kind of fabric during the period of hyperinflation. Years later, strolling through the same strip malls on Santa Fe Avenue where I use to buy mine, none of the backpacks said "Made in Argentina." I must have bought it on some trip during winter break when I would come visit my aunt's house in Buenos Aires. My aunt lived two blocks away from Congress, and my mom would give me a hundred *australes* to buy whatever I wanted on vacation. Because I was afraid of taking buses, I would walk straight along Callao Avenue until Santa Fe, where I would roam through the strip malls (where there were always cheaper things than they had in the street-facing shops). I used that backpack a lot until it was totally finished. I had sewn it back together a few times before that with a thick needle and white thread. Whenever it got dirty, I washed it with detergent and a toothbrush, and then I'd hang it out on the clothesline on the patio, in the sun. I think I used that one for most of junior high, by the end of which it was uncool to still have a backpack and everybody would just carry all their books with an elastic band around them.

Purses and backpacks always played an important role in my life, which is to say they've always had a place in my heart. When I finished my junior year of high school, I went to live in Europe with a family of strangers in one of those exchange programs that were so popular in the '80s and were probably part of a strategy by the Powers That Be to pave the way for globalization. All of my parents' friends' kids, and even my older brother, had gone or were going to the United States, but America seemed so boring to me, and I insisted they let me go to Europe, *any* country in Europe. A few weeks before my departure, on my sixteenth birthday, they spent a considerable sum buying me everything I would need for the year: shoes, sweaters, jeans, and of course, a bag. It was 1990, the dazzling last decade of the second millennium. To save money, my aunt took me to this place outside the city called Munro, where everything was allegedly a lot cheaper. I bought a black leather jacket with lots of zippers as well as a cloth-and-rubber handbag, also black. It was rectangular with a pocket on the front covered by these bulky little rubber sticks—a design I don't think I've ever seen again. It was in vogue that year, and then it disappeared. You could say it was an "industrial" inspiration, black and impersonal, geometric. A few years later, gray and plaid became trendy, which in my teenage mind was all "futuristic," "avant-garde," "modern," and represented everything I wanted to be at seventeen.

Life with the Belgian family was tricky. We didn't understand each other. As arrogant then as I am now, I thought they were uncultured and had bad taste. After all, they didn't have a home library, they watched too much television without any ironic distance, and they'd celebrated the mother's birthday in a French chateau built for birthday rentals. They had a lot of money, that was true, those smalltime growing industrialists. They had an office furniture factory on a piece of property big enough to hold an industrial plant, their offices, their house, and a stable with two horses for Els, the family's only daughter, to practice *équitation*. I lived in Erick's bedroom. He was their youngest, away on an exchange program living with a family in the United States. In addition to having his room, I was allowed to use his yellow scooter and his extensive collection of backpacks. But I used only one to take my things to school with me. It was a beige Kipling backpack made out of intentionally wrinkled canvas. Midyear, they brought all of the exchange students on a trip to London. We went from France by boat. It was a nice trip. There was a tall, slender East German girl with pale, blushing cheeks and blue eyes, who wore all black. She had her hair dyed red and talked about a type of music called acid house. I recall that, upon hearing the name of this music genre, I felt like I was near something totally fascinating, though I didn't have the slightest clue what it might sound like. I'm trying to remember if, during that trip to London, I bought some kind of bag or backpack, but I don't remember any. I know that in some shopping center (which reminded me an awful lot of the ones on Santa Fe Avenue), I bought a black silk matelassé hoodie and, in a giant department store, a metal pendant with a giant dollar sign plus a velvet beret just like I had seen Lisa Stansfield use on MTV. Oh, how I loved Lisa Stansfield and how I wanted to look like her when I was sixteen. That summer, I traveled by myself with an Interrail pass (which let you travel all over Europe for twenty days for something like twenty dollars), and I think I kept using the same black handbag I had bought in Munro.

Obviously, I didn't think it was so uncool, like everything else I dragged along with me from Argentina, all of which, after a few weeks in the First World, looked worn out, cheap, and dingy. I carried my clothes in a big, camper's bag. One time in a train compartment, I made out with an Argentine boy who wanted to sleep together, but I told him no, 'cause I was a virgin. I had just turned seventeen. Clearly, the boy just wanted sex, and I was free in the world. But I didn't know that men were like that. I didn't know men try to have sex whenever they can. I was so naive.

In 1991, I went back to Mendoza, Argentina, and in '92, I moved to Buenos Aires to study film and literature. I quit film school because working as a filmmaker seemed too bureaucratic. I can't remember what purse or bag I carried around during my first few years of college. I've truly erased that from my memory. I do remember that at some point in the '90s, clear plastic handbags came into fashion. They let you see the bag's entire contents. There was a professor who would have been about forty-two, about the same age that I am now. She was thin with fiery red hair, and she had that kind of bag. Gabriela, the one who was my best friend in college, also had a clear handbag, and at one point, she dyed her hair blue. In the '90s, my mom was a civil servant, and she traveled regularly to other countries. I remember one time when she brought me two Zara purses from Spain, one animal print and the other black (as if imitating a black panther), that I think were like felt, but most likely synthetic. In the '90s, faux fur was fashionable and politically correct. In that decade, I also had a black rubber-like purse shaped like aluminum that closed with two little metal balls like a giant coin purse, a design inspired by the '50s. But to be honest, I can't remember the order of those purses in my life. They're all mixed up in my head now, loose, floating along with my youth.

In 1997, I spent a year living in Seattle, studying at a university there, and I had a Bleu de France backpack for my books. It was completely minimalist, square, gender neutral, with foam filling or something else bland on the back so the books wouldn't hurt your back. Even though I got it pretty cheap, that backpack was great quality and I used it for about ten years, until 2008, when I met Claudio and gave it to him. Then he used it until 2013, when he gave it to Ilsa, the Paraguayan woman who comes once a week to clean my house.

In 1999 came the time when I had what I guess you could call an art gallery with my friend Fernanda where we sold trinkets made in China, art supplies, and used clothes, and had art exhibitions in the basement. Every morning, I took the 168 bus to go open the shop, but I don't remember which purse I used. Maybe it was the blue backpack from Seattle or the 1950s-style black handbag. Because nobody had any money then, nobody (including me) bought anything new. I also remember the bags everybody else had, too, including Fernanda's (my business partner) and the ones that people who came to the gallery had as well. One time, an artist complained that somebody had stolen her wallet from her purse. Her name was Alejandra, and she blamed the theft on this homeless trans woman who Alejandra claimed went to events in the art world just to steal from people. But I don't remember what hers or anybody else's purses were like in 1999.

In 2000, I went to Europe as a guest of a friend I had made in Belgium back in high school. Eefje called me and said, "I'm getting married in London, and I'm going to send you a ticket on British Airways." It was awesome, the kind of thing that only happens to you once in a lifetime, I think. She was marrying a millionaire and sent me a business class ticket. It was the only time in my life that I traveled that comfortably. (I know that now it's pretty standard and a lot of my contacts in the art world travel all the time in first class or business, but I devoted myself to poetry and live much closer to poverty than abundance.) When I got to London, a Rolls Royce with a driver was waiting for me along with my friend and her beautiful Prada purse: burgundy and bluish black, round, almost reminiscent of a gym bag. It was an object with so much character. A few days after being in her home, Eefje told me she wanted to give me her purse. And she also gave me a lot of things she pulled from her closet: three or four Prada, Gucci, and Cacharel bags, some Michael Kors boots, a pleated Veronique Branquinho skirt (which was brand new and I think the only new thing she gave me that day), two Missoni skirts, a green Christian Dior leotard, and a beige-colored Louis Vuitton cape that I still have, but it looks so expensive that I'm scared to wear it. The deal Eefje and I made was that, after she got married, I would stay in London for six months and live with her in an apartment attached to her penthouse so the two of us could write a novel together. It was an outlandish project, given the fact that her native tongue was the Dutch I learned during my time in Belgium that, ten years later, not having heard or read it, I had nearly forgotten. Regardless, after a few weeks, she accused me of "only being there for her money" in a fit of shouts and hand gestures. I told her I wouldn't take that kind of humiliation and was going to Germany where I had a poet friend. Aside from the 2,500 euros in cash that she paid me, the most important thing I took from Eefje's house was the Prada bag. It was smooth and firm with symmetrical lines. Everything fit in it because it was huge, and it never broke. I used it all the time for five years, up until one of its handles broke and a shoemaker in Santiago, Chile, put a piece of black leather between one of the handles and the main leather on the bag to fix it. "I don't have any other color leather," he said, and the purse changed. It started to look very used, even though it was still a Prada.

That Prada now sits in a corner of my closet. I can't work up the nerve to throw it out, because it's the only designer purse I've ever owned in my life.

A Bottle of Vichy Makeup Remover
I Stole from a Poet in Berlin

While taking a bath one Sunday afternoon, I spot the pink bottle, still about three-quarters full: a bottle of Vichy make-up remover that I stole from a poet in Berlin. I've had it for exactly two years now, when I brought it back from Germany in my suitcase. It's so beautiful to fly and bring back things from other continents! Especially Europe, where most things seem to always be of the highest quality. In truth, it's not a "makeup remover." It's *eau moussante nettoyante*—something cleansing or purifying for your skin. And the person I stole it from wasn't a poet, but rather the organizer of a poetry festival I was invited to. I don't really remember what he did for a living. I think he was an economist or a lawyer. We talked about his job when he was driving me from the airport to his apartment in Charlottenburg. He was in charge of the festival's finances. Also, he dressed pretty conservatively. He was always in a shirt and jacket, always black or dark blue. He wasn't even a little gay, but he had a lot of brand-name cosmetics in his bathroom, including that small pink bottle I took. The poor guy, I wonder if he even noticed it was missing or if my theft got lost in the haze of overlooked things. The haze of trivial things. Alright, let's remind ourselves that a pink bottle of makeup remover is, by definition, something trivial, but each time I look at it, I remember that German fall morning when I was frantically searching his house for something to steal as a way of calming my rage. Out of revenge, you could say. And it's strange, because even though I recall with precision the bizarre, delirious moment when, after deciding to take vengeance through theft (and to steal from a European, a.k.a. somebody rich! which made my action not only less vile but even kind of heroic), I opened drawers, closets, and cabinets, guided by a malign frenzy, I can't remember exactly what sparked my indignation. I know that on the night before the reading, we had stuck around in his living room talking with some friend of his after getting back from a dinner they hosted in a neighborhood that used to be part of West Berlin in some sort of 19th-century, French-style mini castle (a "villa," they called it), whose garden they had evidently downsized, as it was now just a small square of grass with some willow or similar-looking tree, between two boring high-rises. During the dinner I realized that the young poets of Berlin or, better put, *that* group of young poets from Berlin, the ones who had organized and were taking part in the festival, was quite conservative. At least culturally. The way the girl who was or at least called herself a poet dressed was conservative. She was also on the organizing committee (and I later found out she was my host's sister and used to live in the apartment where I was staying, which actually belonged to their parents, who now lived in some southern province of Germany). She wore all black velvet clothes, a knee-length skirt, and a blazer, the combination of which came off as extremely conservative to me. It was the combined effect of the cut of the clothes and the material... Maybe velvet alone isn't so conservative, but a blazer? A blazer can't ever be part of a progressive outfit. Furthermore, rock, hip-hop, and pop never came up that night; we only spoke of classical music. Well, in truth, the festival (whose name I've already forgotten) was meant to bring together contemporary classical music and poetry. Thus, half the people at this dinner wouldn't stop speaking about instruments and strange, unique, exclusive, "breathtaking" encounters that had taken place in the English countryside or on some seaside rocky cliff in Scotland—events that indelibly change your life. I was supposed to read over Piazzolla's *The Four Seasons of Buenos Aires*. A bandoneon player from Argentina who had been living in Switzerland since 2002 (after the economic crisis) would play the piece. He seemed to be a rather respected figure. The organizer, his sister, and others close to the organizing committee called him "maestro," "maestro." Furthermore, all of the poets there seemed to really understand contemporary classical music, something that was almost completely foreign to me. And now that I think of it, was that not the source of my resentment? Not belonging to the elegant world of contemporary classical music or really just the world of music in general? Not having experienced that feeling of a force that transforms everything in a way that your life no longer belongs to you and becomes part of the beauty manifested by an instrument that makes the air itself vibrate? I don't know.

After dinner at the villa, Gustav, as my victim was called, offered to take me back to his (that is, my) apartment in his car. A friend of his, who spoke Spanish with a Spaniard's accent, came with us. When we got back to his place, we all sat in his cold living room. In spite of his pretension over having found aesthetic beauty in classical music, Gustav's apartment, I must say, was so bland in terms of décor. It was as if nobody had ever lived in the house or the objects within it weren't objects at all, but rather photo clippings of the boxes those very objects would come packaged in at some store like Ikea or Homecenter. Not to mention the apartment was in one of those complexes of cookie-cutter towers built in the late '90s, the ones you find all over the world without any individuality or local flavor. There, we took up different topics of conversation over a bottle of white wine that I think was left over from the dinner and Gustav brought back from the villa. I remember the breadth of topics we discussed being quite expansive, though I can hardly recall any of them now, for I can't remember more than a thing or two of what was said. For instance, at one point, my host asserted with a hand motion (which I couldn't decipher as a sign of concern or just a neutral gesture in the course of stating a fact) that 70 percent of Afghanistan's population is under 13 years old. I think he was trying to imply that within a few decades, the rest of the world would greatly surpass Europe in terms of population. Now that I'm thinking about it, I don't know how we got on that topic. Conversations are always mysterious, and sometimes, with people from different cultures, I'm not even sure if they're conversations or performances. Later on, we (I was the one who said it) also spoke about how *German* television or really just television in general is stupid. I was referencing a show I'd seen that afternoon during some free time I had before heading to the bandoneon player's rehearsal. On it, people looked at houses and apartments they were considering renting or buying. I'm not sure if I specifically said "German television" (because I'm not totally confident that's what I said, though it's pretty likely) or what, but now, with my gaze fixed on the little pink bottle of *eau moussante nettoyante*, I'm reconsidering the sequences of events. It seems like this may have been the breaking point after which Gustav stopped treating me well and started treating me poorly. Maybe it was because he thought it was in poor taste for me to criticize his country, given I was a guest in the country whose visit was paid for with public and private funds from the most prosperous country in the European Union, the one that decides the fate of the euro. Maybe Germans just don't like it when anybody criticizes Germany, just as nobody likes it when people criticize their country. But at that point, the night took a nosedive. Gustav's friend asked me what I had been writing lately, and I told him that I was thinking of doing something with a thing I heard someone say outside my son's preschool, one of those things moms say while we wait for our children on a narrow Buenos Aires sidewalk. A novel or something, maybe an experimental book, of the things middle-class mothers say worrying about their children, the fights between them, the constant references to status, consumerism, and family life. Things like, "Next month, we're going to Disney!" Or, "Delfi is taking piano lessons." Or, "Martín just got vaccinated at such-and-such doctor's office." After explaining my idea a bit with my clumsy, foreigner's

German (really a mix of German and English), an indignant Gustav said from the kitchen, "Who cares?" He said it in English, I think, for that's a more universal way of saying it. And maybe, for that reason, because he said it in English, with all the weight of the universe that his question held when asked in that language, it hurt even more. It wasn't so much a question as an affirmation of his dislike that was meant to say, "Who even cares about your poetry? Who cares about your life? Who cares that you have a son?" He said it while looking away, lowering his gaze. He didn't even have the courage to look me in my eyes or maintain eye contact for all of three seconds. I tried defending myself, pretending like his comment hadn't hurt me at all. I tried answering him with indifference and insincere cordiality. I said, "What matters in art is not the 'what,' but the 'how.'" Not the what, but the how. *Nicht der was aber der Wie.* But I've already forgotten what else he told me or what I said back to him after that. Or what his friend added, if he even intervened. I went to sleep and when I woke up the next day, Gustav wasn't there anymore. He had left me a halfhearted goodbye note on the kitchen table. My plane was leaving that day, a Sunday, at 2 p.m., and I needed to be at a friend's house by 11 so she could take me to the airport. It was 9, and I needed to pack and take a cab to Eva's. I made myself coffee with his capsule coffee machine and then furiously opened every drawer in his house, thinking of what I could steal from him. Written like that, it sounds terrible. And it is. But something drove me to do it. And when I threw the Vichy makeup remover into my suitcase, I felt like I was doing a good thing. Was I so upset because somebody had questioned something that I thought was a brilliant idea? To be honest, I don't know what the difference is between ideas that are brilliant and ideas that aren't, nor do I know how to transform anger into anything else. If stealing can accomplish it or if it takes something else. I am aware that one of the most difficult things in life is to control our anger, and when I realize that at the grown age of thirty-eight, I did something like this, I wonder if I'll ever be a calm person, if I'll ever change…

It's already been two years since that trip, and I never wrote that book about mothers' voices and stories. (My son finished preschool, and now he's in elementary school. He's learned how to read, multiply, and swim. And mom talk no longer seems interesting to me from a literary perspective.) Truthfully, I've hardly written anything in the past two years, other than this story about Gustav that I'm writing now. Maybe Gustav was right, and art must be something grandiose like a Schubert concert on a rocky cliff, not just some semi-ironic ungrammatical narrative about the trivialities of life.

That was the last time I was in Europe.

Easily Amused

Writing is traveling, sliding, merging, flowing, suffering, dreaming, imagining, becoming intoxicated, and listening to Aspen Radio in a hot bath one Sunday afternoon. They're playing '80s and '90s classics. (We call them the '80s and the '90s, in the plural, which makes sense to me, as I found them to be intense years filled with change, and there were so, so many of them that I felt like I lived multiple lifetimes.) As I bathe with my lavender soap, the lyrics of those legendary songs come over me and, along with the hot water flowing from the faucet, jolt me awake. I then feel the urge to get out of the tub straight away, dry off quickly, and start transcribing the words to a Nirvana song. That compulsive feeling that I must stop what I'm doing and transcribe something happens to me in other scenarios as well.

Whenever I watch TV, especially entertainment news shows, I feel the urge to open my laptop and write down everything that the hosts and guests are saying. It's awful, almost like a sickness. During a time of confusion, I thought this could be a work of art, so I filled up several pages of verse with a showgirl's accusations of abuse against Carmen Barbieri, the owner of the company she worked for.

I can't believe I found that interesting. I never should have bought a television in the first place. But since I already have it, I think perhaps I should forbid myself from watching it whenever those kinds of shows are on, because they're bad for me. If nothing else, they make me waste time: I'm not writing, nor am I making any progress on the book I need to turn in so I can get the second installment of my grant. Now I'm also questioning whether or not it makes sense for me to get grants, as they really give me too much free time to watch those TV shows that take me over like evil forces. It would be better just to lie down and open a book. That's what I should do to feel better, not listen to the radio online or watch TV.

I grab the first volume I find in my library. It's a biography of an Argentine author. At first, I like it. It pulls me in. It tells anecdotes of his childhood and teenage years in a neighborhood on the outskirts of Buenos Aires. But soon, an urge comes over me to throw the book on the ground forcefully to protect myself from the horrifying things that it says. Around page 10, it speaks negatively—*quite* negatively—about a woman. A sex worker. It's not like it says anything specific, but it certainly has a disdainful tone. It discusses a time when the author couldn't perform with a prostitute, but without expressing any compassion for her at all. It merely narrates the author's misery over not being able to get hard. It happens on Corrientes Street in Buenos Aires, and it's disgusting, for there's nothing more chauvinist than a male chauvinist complaining about how he can't get it up. Impotence is the perfect shield for misogyny. As it is, I always wonder whether or not words can convey objective feelings or if projection is the only thing that's real; whether or not what I think words contain within them is just something internal within me. Sometimes I feel like releasing poison into the world, albeit through art, is a bad thing, because it continues to be violent despite being well written. Though I've also thought (because I heard somebody else say it, not because I came up with it) that it's okay for the sake of revealing humans' great diversity of emotional hues and mental states.

Something along the lines of projection happened to me today with that Nirvana song, and it was nice feeling like Kurt Cobain and I were the same person because we were going through the same thing: both of us bored with the world.

It happened to me again this afternoon. After trying to make progress on my book so I could turn it in and then opening up that other book and throwing it on the floor, I went to the produce market to buy some fruit. It's a cool market where you pick out your own fruit, like at a supermarket, and they play the best music (sometimes cumbia, sometimes pop). Today, they were playing "Sussudio" by Genesis, a band I loved growing up but hadn't listened to in awhile. I don't know what the lyrics mean, because "sussudio" is a made-up word. But as I put pears and bananas in my bag, I felt connected to Phil Collins and understood his message: Made-up words—yes, made-up words—they are the key to happiness. (Some day, I'll finish my book using made-up words. I know I will, and I'll receive the second part of my grant.)

Noelle Kocot

It was a late February afternoon. One of those afternoons when the sunlight seems to be growing tired of such a long, hot summer and begins to warm a bit more sporadically, announcing fall's arrival. I was sitting around, tired, when I thought translating poetry could inject a bit more energy into my life. I walked into one of those café-bars downtown, all stately and European, just across the street from the Stock Exchange, and took my laptop out of my rolling backpack. When I don't have anything to do, I like to wander around downtown. I don't really know why. Instead of a purse, I take a wheeled backpack like the ones schoolchildren use. It's so much more comfortable. One of my son's backpacks, which I stole from him.

I ordered a cortado, which, in this old-school café, always comes with a large glass of freshly squeezed orange juice, and I opened a blank document in Word. "I'm going to translate a poem from English," I told myself. "Any old poem, it doesn't matter which. The first one that I find online, though I'd like for it to be contemporary. A poem that's never been translated. I'm going to contribute something to the world as a translator of poetry." I recalled that the night before, I had met a very tall man with curly, blonde hair from California who mentioned "Noelle Kocot." His favorite poet, he said. This man, a perfect stranger, had walked into a bookstore in Palermo for singer Francisco Garamona's book release party at exactly the same time as me. And for some reason of fate that I couldn't explain to you, we stopped on the same step, looked each other in the eyes, and he said, "You must read Noelle Kocot."

Now that I think about it, I'm not sure if that's how it really happened or if desire has wildly distorted my mental impression of that moment. My desire to flee Argentina and marry a tall, blonde foreigner like him. But that's another story, and this afternoon, in that café across the street from the Stock Exchange, while other patrons discussed the price of the "blue dollar," the "blue chip swap," and other issues of economic speculation, I typed "Noelle Kocot" into Google and found a fantastic poem called "While Writing." It started:

> *Someone inside says, "Get busy."*
> *But I've got appointments to keep,*
> *I have an abstemious love of equations calculated quickly*
> *While the tepid day melts into design.*

Translating the first stanza was easy. Where it says "equations calculated quickly," I thought of saying, "ecuaciones calculadas en un flash." I thought "flash" sounded better because of the musicality of the "sh" sound. (A more direct translation of "quickly" as "rápidamente" would have ruined the poem.) Having by chance found this text containing that specific verse, which so precisely described the scene surrounding me at that moment, in the infinite sea of the Internet made me curious about the poet that wrote it. At the end of the day, the only thing I knew about her was her name. I remembered that Stuart also had given me her email. It was on a small scrap of paper in the pocket of my jeans.

Obviously, poetry isn't like rock music. Poets don't have fans or followers. I didn't want to bother Noelle Kocot's peaceful life in Brooklyn. But I was dying to write her and ask more about her and her life. What time she wakes up, if she writes by hand in a notebook or types directly on her computer, if she plays sports or smokes heavily, whether or not she likes fruit… Around me, the men (because they were almost all men) kept talking ever more fervently about money, numbers, percentages, bonds, euros, dollars… They hardly even mentioned the peso. And that was all I had in my wallet: Argentine pesos. I only had 32 pesos left, enough to pay for my cortado and take the A line on the subway back home to Once, the neighborhood where I live. But first, I wanted to finish translating the poem. It was something I had taken on and needed to finish. Just because. No particular reason. Translating because quickly calculated equations were surrounding me, and my life needed to change. The poem went on:

> *And the high cheekbones of the beautiful life*
> *Bear the loose look of a calendar by lamplight.*
> *I search for patterns in everything.*
> *I am tied in knots of comprehension.*

"Los altos pómulos de la bella vida…" What a marvelous verse! I also wanted my life to be like a Norwegian model with well-defined cheekbones and silky-smooth hair. Yes, Noelle Kocot was right. Life had to be like that: like a beautiful person. And I had to chase after knots of comprehension, links of lucidity. But how could I be a translator of poetry and have a perfect life? Is it possible to have a beautiful life without money? And what could I do to get money? I obviously would never march into the Stock Exchange to buy up shares. I could sell my apartment and invest the money to earn back double, and then buy a house in a nicer neighborhood and waste the rest of the money on eating out… but I was fairly certain I would never bring myself to do something like that. You need to love numbers to do that, and I hate numbers. When I was 7 years old, I discovered poetry in a shrub full of white flowers, and I definitely felt that my life would forever be devoted to looking for those moments of beauty. I was on my way home from school, walking back after the first day of classes in second grade, and I was certain those flowers had the same beauty as snow. My childish heart cried of happiness.

I was already almost done translating "While Writing," and I thought about posting it on Facebook. I searched online for Noelle Kocot's precise year of birth so I could credit her, but I couldn't find it anywhere. It wasn't listed on any of her book flaps or in any of the hundreds of online magazines that spoke about her work, so I decided to send her an email. I asked for her year of birth and if I had her permission to share her poem in Spanish. She answered, saying of course I could post the poem and that she had been born in Brooklyn. I wrote back insisting for her date of birth, and she once again answered with her city of birth. Evidently, she had a problem with numbers. Numbers, the cruelest way to measure time—and she had erased them from her life. She didn't even remember how old she was anymore. It didn't really make a difference whether she had forgotten her or just didn't want to reveal it. But now I knew for sure that Noelle Kocot could become my guru and guide my initiation. Into what? I don't know. But I wanted to and needed to be initiated. Deep down, any poet we like is our guru, and if not, why else would we read poetry? Whenever I read Paul Valéry's "The Graveyard by the Sea," I feel like I must commit myself fully to his worship. Not having any God, I can turn Paul Valéry into my God for five minutes while sitting at a café table. It doesn't make a difference if Paul Valéry is alive or dead. Noelle Kocot is alive, though I can't estimate how much longer she will be. Maybe she's already 130 years old, and she's an avatar of light that has remained in her cozy Brooklyn apartment meditating. Maybe some day I'll be able to visit that borough and kiss her hand and be initiated by her. The poem ends:

> And that after marching one doozy of a kilometer after another,
> We each come upon the same poem scribbled in invisible ink
> Taped to the door of a room
> In which an austere justice is burning for us.

*Y después de marchar un espléndido quilómetro
tras otro*
*todos daremos con el mismo poema garabateado en
tinta invisible*
*pegado con cinta en la puerta de una habitación
en la que una justicia austera arde por nosotros.*

I Want to Be Fat

Everybody deserves to be fucked.
—Sex in Dallas

Feeling (with a capital "F") is something so complex that it must be crafted and manifested delicately and rigorously. That's why my girlfriends and I have invented a drug to help us feel. New things. And feeling new things helps us change. We call it "Disturbance," but only cause we had to name it something, and that was the closest word at hand. But it doesn't have anything to do with what you think of when you hear that word. It doesn't bear any relation whatsoever to the idea of causing public uproar or conflict. We don't take to the streets to cause trouble. It's really more about an internal disturbance achieved through strategic outings to the external environment (which, at the end of the day, is intertwined with the inside on a quantum level). What we're after is feeling undiscovered emotions, and we try achieving this through a "foam rubber drug" (if you asked me to summarize what it is). Although, as far as I'm concerned, I don't think you can describe the chemical processes happening in my neurons so simply.

Namely, we dress up in fat suits to perceive the world from that place. When you're fat, men don't try to seduce you. And that is a kind of freedom. Every Friday, at 9 o'clock, five of my friends and I gather at my house: Marina, Gabriela, Fernanda, Natalia, Carolina, and me. By the time they arrive, I've already set up pizza and chocolates on the kitchen counter. That's how we start our excursion: eating those (forbidden) foods in large quantities. We gather round the kitchen table, and as we eat, we say women's names aloud: Ada, Gema, Benita, Luz, Elma, Jacinta, Delmira, Domitilia, Federica, Marión. Original names that we all wish we had, even just for a little while. Because we don't want to abandon our identity forever. Just for a few hours. (Just as we also don't wish to abandon our bodies definitively—just a few hours are enough to change.)

Once we finish eating, we head to my bedroom to disrobe. My friends are all tidy, and they fold their clothes on the chairs that I arrange around the bed. Each chair has a sign with a name. That way, when we come back home, euphoric and in an altered state of consciousness, we more easily recognize the women we were and the clothes we wore before going out.

Then I take out a plastic box full of sheets of foam rubber and scissors, and we get to work. We cut out rectangles and circles, which we bind to ourselves with clear string: on our arms, our legs, our neck, and our core. We try to make sure that not an inch of real skin stays visible. We saturate our body with foam rubber until we become truly huge people. Bombastic, padded beings. Once fat, we paint the material with a rosy pink paint. Finally, we get dressed. We choose clothes with bold colors to call more attention to ourselves (and also because women's magazines always have articles advising against gaudy colors because they make you look fat). (In general, our motto is to do the opposite of whatever women's magazines say to do.)

Around midnight, we hit the streets with our new bodies and our new personalities. We take a cab and spend the night roaming, going in and out of restaurants, bars, bookstores, record shops, and any other places that speak to us. We sit on the concrete benches in city parks, each of us lined up with our spongy hips rubbing against one another's and our arms around each other to form one continuous mass or train of flesh. Or we move and sway, spreading out on a dance floor under the strobe lights.

We spend hours feeling fat in the city. Not just fat women holed up in our apartments, but fat women roaming in the aristocratic, well-lit streets of well-to-do neighborhoods. Those are the neighborhoods we like visiting most. All the women there are slender and wear toned-down colors: black, brown, navy-blue, moss green, gray… And the drug of fatness is much more effective when experienced through contrast. By stepping into these scenes, we feel like real freaks.

And let me tell you, there's no drug as powerful as the gaze of your neighbor when it raises you up to the avant-garde level of feeling like a freak. Nobody really knows anything about life until they've felt, even for a split moment, under any circumstances, like they're a freak. Until the way others looked at you gave you more of an adrenaline rush than jumping off a bridge or taking ecstasy and dancing all night at a rave ever could. And once you've had a taste of it, it's hard to stop. We're sure that when we're older, we're going to want to be like those women who die their hair every week, so it's fried and blonde, but a tasteless, streaky kind of blonde, wearing gaudy makeup with exaggerated lips drawn on, and sweatpants with heels, and worn-out, sequined sweaters, and purple sunglasses—those women you see on the bus and think, "I wanna look like her when I'm 60." But now, at 30, our only option is to be fat.

Once we've had enough, around 4 or 5 a.m., we grab a cab home. On our way back, we try to put into words what we've just experienced. We take out notebooks and quickly jot down our impressions (like Baudelaire did with hash). Later, during the week, we edit and revise our notes and send them to each other in emails. The world is changing, and now is the time to invent new experiences. People have already tried every drug on the market, and they need to find new ones. Because the most important thing is to change. And drugs are the only things that help you change.

Nuns, the Utopia of a World without Men

Carolina said, "Let's be nuns. Let's go live in a convent." I thought for a second, mulling it over. And then I said, "Yes." Nuns are strange. They're like absentees. They live without men and don't have any troubles in the world. And what's more, I was in a nunnery once, and they always make jokes. They have a great sense of humor. They live in a kind of eternal bliss.

The morning that we left for our future lives, the clouds looked like rocks and the sky was a violent purple shade. Children were hiding behind their mothers' skirts, frightened of the strange light looming over the day. It was a gloomy winter morning, and we held hands, wearing novice's sweaters and fur-lined boots.

We took a long-distance bus with reclining seats that had white paper sheets over them like in a hospital. The trip was quite long, as the convent was off in the countryside, far away from civilization. We spent the ride listening to music on our Walkman. It seemed like a good way to say goodbye to the world. In the middle of the night, while everyone was asleep and you could see the stars through the frosted windows, I tried praying, but I couldn't do it. I don't know why I was going off to become a nun when I couldn't even pray.

We arrived on a clear morning. The clouds from the day before had dissipated. Maybe it's always like this in the countryside. The doors of the convent were like doors on a castle, and the beige walls looked like the walls of a fort. We knocked, both afraid and eager at the same time, and heard steady footsteps inside. The mother superior received us with open arms, flooding our hands and cheeks with kisses. She must have been about 40 years old. Her face was round. Her hair, graying and so long that it crept out of her stiff headpiece.

"Now I'll show you your future home," she said, having us follow her. The convent was made up of many rooms—all dark, cold, and mysterious—connected by hallways. In the distance, you could hear what seemed to be the sound of a piano. But it was just an illusion. The only instrument allowed in the convent was the voice. The naked voice and the accompaniment of palms.

The room she assigned us to share was small and painted blue-green. The color reminded us of the tropics, and we were content. We opened the closet doors wide and stared in rapture at the paintings of the Virgin hanging from each of the four walls. We fell onto our narrow beds, which were side-by-side, though separated by a nightstand. The bedspreads were identical: pink satin with embroidered frills. We lay down, overwhelmed by the exhaustion of the trip, and for a few seconds, we remained very still, almost without even breathing.

"So why did you come?"

"I don't really know. You?"

"Me neither. I think just because you told me to."

"Ah, right... It was that night in a bar. You were upset over a fleeting love. I didn't want to work anymore. And I felt so frustrated... like I needed to get far away from everything. We both thought it sounded like a good idea, because immediately we knew that the convent would bring us purity and calm. We were over Buenos Aires, cause everyone there is a bit annoying. And of course, the Virgin..."

"I like the Virgin a lot. I've always liked her, because I feel like she's happy."

"I love her, especially how they paint her cheeks. She always has porcelain skin, and I don't think she really has any eyelashes."

The next day started really early. For our jobs, we were assigned to take care of the vegetable garden. And we had arrived just in time for the harvest. Potatoes, tomatoes, and cucumbers. We had to harvest all three with our bare hands, which were scant used to the roughness of agricultural work. But we didn't mind, because we no longer had a boss, and the country air and the songs of the birds were revitalizing. We worked so much that morning and so hard that we started to bleed. At first, we didn't even realize, but then I noticed that the basket where we were collecting the potatoes we laboriously pulled from the earth had red stains. They were from our hands! We were both bleeding at the same time. We tried to lick each other's cuts. I took off my shirt, ripped it in two, and made bandages to dress our wounds so we could keep working. Then, a few minutes later, the mother superior, on her way to supervise us, walked up. I was naked and startled, and I thought she might scold me. She looked at my naked chest, causing me to blush. I covered my face in shame, but she was understanding. She drew closer, gently putting her arm around my shoulder and kissing my cheek with her lovely lip. "You shan't be ashamed of your body. The body ends quickly, but is indeed a precious stone," she said. These were her teachings.

That was how the first day of work went.

After gardening came the time for prayer. In the chapel, on our knees, we were supposed to meet God. On our first day, they told us that once we were ready, we would marry Him.

In bed at night, staring at the ceiling, I asked Carolina if it had ever occurred to her that we both would be marrying the same man: a quite unusual arrangement, one that would never happen in Buenos Aires. Something unique to the convent that would never be allowed at the civil registry. And she kissed me. Our love grew stronger as we thought about the fate that we'd share the same Father-Husband, who would love us both equally and always open his Kingdom of Light to us without asking of us anything in return.

Strange things happened in the convent at night. You could hear muted footsteps coming from the hallways, like people coming and going on tiptoes from one cell to another.

Sometimes, in the mornings during breakfast, small clusters of nuns whispered amongst themselves. Or one nun might rest her head on another's shoulder in a caring gesture. Or they would hold hands under the table. Some of the nuns were in love with one another, and they didn't hide it. It was quite sweet. One night, I also thought about experiencing the intensity of sex. As I went to brush my teeth after a long day of work, Sister Paula approached me from down the convent's narrow hallway. Sister Paula was very organized. I had admired the cleanliness and symmetry of everything in her life: her drawers, her sheets, her pillows—everything immaculate, everything sparkling clean. She had fallen for me, as I would later find out, though I don't know why. She had fallen for me, the messiest girl in the convent. Me, who wrote "I <3 disorder" twenty times on a single page of my diary. She calmly approached me. (What I loved about that place was that everything—the people, the furniture, the spaces—was so calm.) She didn't say anything or greet me in any way. She stared at me, and I returned her gaze. We remained still as we stared deep into each other's eyes, face-to-face, motionless. My breath quivered, and she drew closer and kissed my lips. I didn't pull back. A pleasant half-light reigned over us. She placed her hands on my breasts and touched them softly. We drew even closer to one another. I could feel her heavy vestments, the heavy fabrics covering her up. I loved how she wore so many articles of clothing. Because they smelled nice, like lavender. The clothes fit tightly. The gray twill weave framed her bust and hips. I ran my hands along her clothes. Beneath her skirt, she had on three underskirts that were smooth and silky. I put one hand between her legs and could feel her wet plush underwear. That heat and moistness startled me. This was unchartered territory. It felt like moving forth toward my own pleasure and seeing it by the light of day, blinding me on a sweltering, terrestrial afternoon. From that point on, I felt nothing else, had no more thoughts. I felt the urge. I wanted to press firmly against her like a forceful mare, to grab her waist, to bite her. I felt like she was my toy, my doll. I pushed her down to the floor and let myself fall on top of her. Our breasts pressed together. Our nipples brushed. And she was like an elephant, with smooth, soft skin, an everlasting heat, perdition in the grotto of love.

"I don't have a lot of experience with girls," I told her. She didn't answer. I unbuttoned her dress slowly. I was so aroused and instinctively took off my underwear and started touching myself. She grabbed my ass, pulling my pussy against hers and rubbing against me. It was like real sex. Her pussy was so smooth and warm against mine. I felt like I was enjoying every inch of it, not like when men would stick it in me, which always hurt a little and made it hard to cum. With men, orgasms were light. With Paula, my orgasm was almost endless. Afterwards, we both stood up, each going our separate ways, though not without hugging each other first and feeling the heat of each other's hearts. I wonder what Carolina is up to? "The infinite love of people is infinite," I thought.

Carolina was asleep. I don't know what she was dreaming about, but she was tossing from side to side. I got into bed and looked her way. Sometimes, proximity to other people upsets me. But being around Carolina never does. Because she is good like a basket of angels and joyful like a sleigh bell. Even though we've never slept together, with her I've been to Paradise.

A Post-Marxist Theory of Unhappiness

Everything I write is based off of something that one of my girl-friends told me. I never experienced any of this. I've never been married. Never had any lovers. I've never flirted with someone on the Internet, nor have I ever picked anyone up at a club or anywhere else really, either. From a young age, I knew my life would be devoted to writing, and because of that, I would never have a normal dating life. But the world changed so quickly, and from one day to the next, nobody had a normal dating life any-more. Like that, I stopped being weird and became just another one of the hundreds of thousands of people who have renounced monogamy. Just like that, my life slowed down. Or started to fly by. (At this point, it's hard to tell which.) And I let myself fall into that slowness (or speed)—and it was soft, as if a down comforter were there to break my fall. And I fell...and fell, and fell, and fell, like in an ad for chocolate. And imme-diately, the comforter reassumed its intended purpose, and I wrapped myself up in the warmth of that nest and stayed there forever: at home. Or in literature, which was essentially the same thing, for within the walls of my house, the words of others lived and were given life anew. Undoubtedly, the best literature isn't in books; it's in the lives of the people we know.

I find everything that my girlfriends tell me interesting, regardless of whether or not it's about love. Though most of the time, it is about love. What else is there to talk about? Is there any other topic of conversation that doesn't lead back to love? Politics maybe, but nobody can make sense of that anymore. From the soft swaying of a beechwood rocking chair I inherited from my grandmother back when there was still enough fuel to run the world, I take in the city and talk on the phone. This is how I spend my days, and I'm happy. But it's a question of originality. I'm not that different from the rest of humanity in that respect, either. The truth is that there isn't much else to do but converse (other than falling in love, of course). The world is running out of its supply of energy, and everything is changing at the speed of a hurricane. There are very few industries left, for example, and the labor market has ceased to exist altogether. Although we still have the objects of the past, we're aware that once they deteriorate and stop serving a purpose, we will not be able to replace them, with the exception of the tools we use to communicate with one another. The world government has decided that until an alternative energy source is discovered or invented, we will use every remaining barrel of petroleum to make computers, cell phones, and satellite dishes.

And love flows unhindered through computers, cell phones, and satellite dishes. This is the most beautiful part of the future, because not only did the plastic shortage change the world, but there has also been an incredible change in people's dating lives. For instance, nobody wants to get married anymore. Or have kids either. (And that's why, like I said before, although I never got married, I'm not a rare species, just a completely average person.) And if somebody did decide to get married, they couldn't do it anyways, because the State no longer acts as the guarantor for such associations. Nobody understands what the exact connection is between the two (for social sciences have also ceased to exist), but industry has disappeared, taking marriage along with it. People no longer want their bonds to be eternal; they want to change, expand, wander. Because of this, couples last about two-and-a-half years on average, which scientists have now decreed the norm from a biological perspective. Hormones dictate these things. Religion has vanished from the face of the earth. And although deep down some older people still have feelings that are remnants from the old order—archaic ones, such as jealousy—instances of those feelings are becoming less and less common. (If a woman or man were to show jealousy in public, it would be nearly impossible for anybody else to ever love them again.) Or the feelings have mutated and become similar, yet adapted versions of those primitive emotions. Lighter, more porous versions. Less tragic or hurtful, and therefore, far more interesting, you could say. Emotions closer to the infinite—society's new quest. For example, there can be jealousy between partners, but the emotion is no longer triggered by something as crude as possession. Instead, it has to do more so with geometry, social glamour, the happiness of the moment—all things that, in the old era, would have been considered as insignificant as one's sense of fashion. In all social strata, there's a frenzy to be fashionable, to play that game of coding and decoding subtle meanings through one's articles of clothing. But unlike what used to happen in the era of consumerism, today there are no longer boutiques. All clothes are made from alterations of old clothes that get traded over and over again between friends and neighbors. There was so much clothing left in the world when all the fuel ran out that they'll last long enough to dress everyone for centuries. Therefore, men and women have learned to sew, and the antiquated jealousy that couples used to feel isn't based exclusively on the beauty of clothing or the amount of praise one receives when they walk out in public with a certain style. This new kind of jealousy is comparable what was known in the old era as "career envy" between spouses, except this newer version no longer has to do with success, that is, one's potential future (effectively because jobs no longer exist, nor do such concepts as accumulation or the future), but with the present: One must shine here and now. It's like a requirement.

To shine here and now. To dazzle. To wrap yourself up in a symphony of shapes, in the softness of the fabric, which sooner or later ends up playing hide-and-seek with your skin. Or as the 20th-century designers said all the time, to wear it like your second skin. That's the main point: It's all about acquiring, any way you can, a second skin. Thus, shapes and colors glide over our bodies like an aura. Above all, this awakens a sense of fascination within us. Fashion has assumed a central role in our social organization. So much so that finding a partner depends almost exclusively on the clothes you wear. And clothes are no longer a thing that will just inevitably end up on the floor, but a central part of any relationship. It's taken centuries, but people finally understand that love isn't something between two people, and even less so something that is decided in bed. Love is a complex balance of the countless signs and feelings that make us live, and those signs are as integral a part of us as are our hair color or the cut of the skirt we're wearing. For decades, humanity had to put up with a strange increase in nudity. For some as yet unexplained reason (as I said before, social sciences and psychology no longer exist), in the last decades of the 20th century, several generations of human beings came and went, all convinced that the limits of who they were as people were their own body's limits and that being nude was more "natural." Today we know that, in reality, we're nothing more than an extension of the objects we use or just another stage of an endless dialectical game between human beings and inanimate—or semi-animate—objects. Furthermore, today we no longer consider ourselves at all similar to what in the past was called a subject. (Subject to what?) There is no longer anybody who feels isolated or stuck in their own head, as many people felt in centuries past. We are all connected by invisible links, because the second-most important thing after fashion is conversation. We believe that the infinite exists in language and that language, just like fashion, doesn't belong to anybody; anyone can use it. It doesn't matter what somebody says or who says something. What matters is the scintillating, musical shade that the words in a conversation cast upon space. That is, in this world, here and now, content no longer exists; only form matters.

Infidelity, for example, doesn't exist. Well, it exists, but only as a topic of debate. Incidentally, today at 3 p.m., Gabriela called me, and we spoke for a few hours. She told me that she had discovered her grandmother's diary, where her grandmother wrote all about the affairs she had behind her husband's back. Gabriela said that reading it made her feel nostalgic.

"By no means do I mean to say that I'm interested in betrayal," she said. "This isn't about that, although there was one thing my grandmother wrote that I liked a great deal, and I copied it down because it sounded so passionate even though I'm not entirely sure what it means. 'Love only flourishes in unfaithful soil.' Incidentally, the next time we get together, we could play a game where we search through our ancestors' libraries and find phrases we don't entirely understand, but still sound good, and we can read them to one another. It sounds like a lot of fun. Anyway, getting back to what I was saying. What I longed to feel (all the while knowing that I never will feel it) was that passion with which women in the past were unfaithful. That feeling of doing something new and exciting. Reading my grandmother's diary left me with the impression that women were always getting ready to cheat. As if marriage were a secondary concern and their various secret relationships were their main focus. They did it guilt-free, even though they feigned feeling guilt to avoid facing the moral condemnation they had to face. And they weren't thrilled by it simply because it was forbidden—an overly simplistic explanation. Nor did they do it to get their husbands' attention, as people used to believe. No, being unfaithful didn't carry all those negative connotations. For our grandmothers, infidelity was nothing more than a superficial tool. An artifact without specific attributes they used for various means according to their needs at any given moment in time. Something imbued with new meaning each time it reoccurred. And they did it for themselves and nobody else. I'll read an excerpt:

"When I walked into X's apartment, I knew that my afternoon was stopping in time. The cramped, cozy space, the view of the river, the silence—so distinct from my own—the simple borders on the wallpaper, the distant echoes, like the roar of a train, the pearl on the handle of those spoons we used to sweeten our coffee, the intoxicating scent of bath soap... I could continue with this list for an eternity or write it a thousand times over, because when I cross the threshold of his house, time becomes winding, softer, and those sensations are ingrained within me in such a particular way. I treasure his belongings; I treasure being able to possess the atmosphere of his belongings, albeit for mere hours. Minutes later, this sensation fades away, but it beats on, latent in some part of me and accompanying me at every moment, as if a second, parallel time had taken possession of my heart, as if I could unfold and be two María Luisas—the same and yet, different.

"I find it curious that my grandmother spoke more about belongings and atmospheres than her lover. I read the diary from start to finish, trying to find details about this mysterious 'X,' trying to find some kind of description of his personality or physical features or how he moved, but it was all in vain.

Which leads me to believe that the love she felt for him was actually what mattered least in their relationship. That her infidelity served a purpose other than love. And what she sought by visiting different men's houses—of this, I'm certain—was to multiply time. To multiply the houses. Change the spaces. Coat these multiplicities with affect. She called this 'possessing the atmosphere.' Without a doubt, my grandmother sought out the infinite in an era where it didn't exist. And infidelity was just a gateway to infinity. It's hard for us to understand, because we live in sporadic times, a period bound by desire, with nothing before or after, a time that unfolds with intermittences from the moment we're born until we die. However, for our grandmothers, time was a law. They had to measure and keep watch over the days and hours, the weeks and months. And marriage was one of the most stable ways of organizing that time. That is why women (and the rest of humanity, too) required certain practices to experience the ethereal sensations that for us today constitute our normal lives."

I silently thought about what Gabriela said for a few minutes, and then I told her that I understood exactly what she meant.

"For our grandmothers, infidelity was a means of achieving freedom, which is really just a mode of experiencing time. Now that time is erratic, we're all free. But in 1996, they still had such notions as solidity and eternity. They even got married with the ritual phrase: ''til death do us part.' It's absurd to think that such a torture could be in any way related to love. On the other hand, you have to keep in mind that this fixation with eternity clearly led to the thrill of change. This must have been the case for 99 percent of marriages."

"Perhaps my grandmother believed—or, who knows, she just wanted to believe—in the possibility of annulling the past, of forgetting. Those 'atmospheres' she speaks of are also a way of erasing memories. A sophisticated kind of drug. While she was with her lover, memories of her husband disappeared like magic. Why should she have to put up with this whole narrative in life that marriage thrust upon her? Years with the same man in the same places. Years with the same sayings said under the same exact circumstances. No matter how happy those moments may have been, why should she have to bind herself to them like a mark on her biography? She had to escape. It was just a matter of formalities. Today we understand; we live to escape and wander and start over."

At this point, as we got fired up, Gabriela reminded me that I had never fallen in love. But she didn't say it reproachfully or to try and discredit my argument (nobody believes experience has greater value than speculation), but simply to prolong the chat such that our lively words would continue on until dusk.

"Considering you never fell in love, what do you think of somebody who moves on to a new lover every two weeks?"

"I think those transitions must be painful. And that's why I'm sure monogamy won't last much longer. Everything points in the same direction. I really don't get why that kind of love has such a great reputation. Although on the other hand, perhaps it will stick around. Monogamy doesn't fit into my life, which is built around happiness. And so far, I don't feel like I'm making a mistake. My way of loving is based wholly on epistolary exchanges. Starting a monogamous relationship would make me feel like I'm betraying an ideal. Through letters, seduction is infinite. And this gives me peace of mind. Did women have the freedom to write so many letters in our grandmothers' time?

"It's really hard to know what men back then thought and felt, because the male gender is what has changed the most with time. While women have held onto most of the same characteristics we've always had, men lost so many of their attributes and developed characteristics that used to only exist latent in their psychic structure."

"They stopped being aggressive."

"And became more protective."

"Now it seems inconceivable, but in the past, men had a hard time showing their feelings. It was hard for them to say short, simple phrases expressing life's most essential emotions in a direct way. I'll read you a diary passage that illustrates this perfectly: 'When we finish making love, Juan Carlos is silent as though he had nothing to say. I look off to the side and sigh. Those magical words he hardly ever says fall like raindrops in my heart and mind: I love you, I love you, I love you. At the very least, I say them myself, as if to conjure their absence in him.'"

"Poor woman. It had to be terrible to love somebody like that."

"Maybe she no longed loved him, but had to keep living with him. There's another part where she talks about how her husband traveled (you already know that back then they traveled a lot, especially the husbands), and he would call her on the phone to tell her he'd arrived safely, and not once did he say 'I miss you.' Or, if he did say it, it was never spontaneous. It always sounded like it came out of obligation."

"I wonder why she stayed married to him."

"I have no idea."

"She doesn't explain it in her diary?"

"Nope."

At this point, we stopped speaking and both, without saying goodbye, decided to end the conversation. The custom of ending a phone conversation without saying goodbye is fairly new, and there are people who still get offended when you do it, which seems ridiculous to me. After all, what does a formal greeting add? Absolutely nothing. Today, we tell each other "I love you" a hundred times, but we never say "goodbye." There's so much more merit in perceiving the desire to cease conversation in the cadence of the tone of the person with whom you're speaking than in pronouncing those empty words, in simply sensing that moment when it's time to close your mouth and move on to something else.

Michelle Mattiuzzi

I can never manage to clean the whole house at once. I always clean by room. Then, in the interim between each room and the next, everything gets dirty and messy again, and the house goes back to looking like a tornado ran through it. My house always looks like a hurricane wrecked it just five minutes ago. For many years now, I've felt like my house is a monster to be tamed. Last year, I spent the tail end of winter and almost all of spring remodeling the patio and redoing the backyard with a landscapist from a British family who studied gardening in London. Her name, like mine, was Cecilia. She would come a few days of the week around, say, 3 p.m. I couldn't just sit around watching her do all the work, so I'd get up and help her out. We moved the planters together and also patched up the walls with yellow lime plaster.

And the house changed completely. Because yellow is a powerful color, and now that the backyard has been land-scaped (though it's quite wild—like a jungle), it has become a utopia of calm.

Now I know that some day, though I may never success-fully tame my house, my backyard will give me peace.

I wonder if this idea of taming a house is universal, something all people feel. How do others think about their houses? I'd love to read a book of testimonials about people and their fondness for their living space. I love my house with an almost supernatural love, but I'm not sure if the man I live with feels the same way. His only responsibility is washing the dishes. I do everything else. It's a rule that came about almost tacitly at a time when he was going through a depressive episode. A breakdown, you could call it. And things never changed, even after his psychiatrist discharged him. Now, this is how we divide the chores: He washes all the dishes in the morning, before going to work, and I clean the rest of the house in whatever pockets of time my activities leave me. Because I work from home, and I love it. At one point, somebody lent me their small office downtown so I could focus more on my poetry, but I couldn't get anything done. I would sit in front of the computer, my mind blank, as the minutes passed. After several hours without writing even a single line in the blank document before me, I would get on the subway and come back to my corner at home, next to the washing machine and the stove, where I've been writing for the last fifteen years and where I've written all of my books. Now I'm realizing my poems are also made up of my house, even if they're about love and disappointment. My house is in my heart, and it is *she* who is my muse—not the man I live with, as one would naturally suppose.

Last night, we invited four friends over for dinner. It was definitely our last barbecue this year, because soon the weather won't let us stay outside as late as we did last night. It's 11 a.m., and my husband and I just got out of bed. In the sink, there is an endless pool of grease-stained dishes, as well as six bowls with dried, crusted chocolate ice cream (Pablo brought two quarts of ice cream) and three or four glazed platters we used to bring the raw meat out to the grill and the cooked meat back inside. Everything needs to get washed. It isn't a detestable scene for me. Washing dishes reminds me that my house was full of people—people who laughed and danced in my yard. I have a theory that those happy moments gradually build up, unseen, on the walls, forming a kind of sediment of love that transforms spaces and elevates them. The same thing happens at the birthday and Halloween parties I throw for my son. The patio gets covered in sticky candy and gum, which need to be scraped off afterward and attract teensy, tiny ants overnight. Those dark soda stains on the red stones take weeks to fade away, but I feel like once the patio is impeccable again, the house has somehow evolved. And what's more, I love the foam from the dish soap covering the cups. It makes me feel clean... pure... cleansed.

I don't know if the man who lives with me feels the same way that I do. It's already a quarter past eleven, and he's just starting his share of the cleaning ever so slowly. He washes two forks, three mugs, and then he makes himself coffee. He sits down in the living room armchair to read international news on his phone. Whenever he can, he reads world news. Every so often, he says something about Donald Trump or the British prime minister, Theresa May, or something a little more approving about Putin. I answer with whatever seems pertinent. (I've never been to Russia, and I can't imagine what the Russian mind is like, the Russian way of seeing the world...) In truth, I think of these conversations as what they call "small talk" in English. I'm not that interested in geopolitics, but I do like talking with the man who lives with me.

By half past noon, I've cleaned the bathroom, mopped the patio, and swept and mopped the living room, yet a good 80 percent of the dishes remain in the sink. I say something. "C'mon, what's the deal? You're taking forever to wash three dishes."

I think he then realizes how little time he's got left, and he starts washing everything in a rush: without any love. It's getting close to when he needs to leave for work. He writes essays about art for an Italian magazine. His prose is elegant and refined, with highbrow adjectives you always forget to use and clear conclusions based on ironclad logic. But, when he finishes washing the dishes, he *never* cleans the grease sludge in the sink or the food that builds up in the drain stopper that I got to keep the pipes from getting clogged. All he has to do is take the stopper out and bang it against the side of the trashcan. Apparently, it's a task that the man I live with—a reader of international newspapers—is incapable of doing.

But I'm also a worldly woman. Last year, I was invited to Rio de Janeiro as a translator for an art workshop. There, I met a Black performance artist. In one of the videos she showed, she could be seen walking through Bahia dressed in all white wearing one of those drain stoppers like a muzzle covering her mouth. She stopped once she was in front of the giant iron head of a monument to Zumbi, where she had people stick needles in every part of her face. She was bleeding and crying, but remained still. I think it was the most interesting thing I saw in the whole workshop. There was another artist from the Northeast, an adherent of Candomblé, who shared how she had done a ritual cleansing of a British anthropology museum full of pieces stolen during the colonial era. But her work didn't leave as big of an impression on me. The one with the drain stopper really spoke to me, as it made me think about my house and the man I live with. Sure, I was staying in a beautiful hotel across from Tiradentes Plaza, but they were what I missed. And that night, after seeing Michelle Mattiuzzi's work, I went back to my hotel room and got on Skype to talk with the man I live with. I felt like I missed the drain stopper, too. Full of grease and gross leftovers. As if the dirtiest, most disgusting part of my house was also a part of my heart.

The Gray Journal

Last Saturday, I went to visit my friend Juliana in her studio. After opening the door and welcoming me in for a beer, she took out a huge journal with a gray cover and said, "I got us this journal so we could write something together."

Today, riding the 64 bus and watching the sky—heavy with humidity and weighed down by gray clouds, I thought about the gray journal. I recalled what we started to jot down together the week prior. Juliana and I were in total harmony. I'd write a fragment and hand it to Juliana. She'd continue, then pass it back to me, and we went back and forth like that until we had finished "something." Something I can't define easily, but still hope is literature.

We were together like that for three or more hours, on the edge of ecstasy, as our handwritten letters were cast perfectly onto the manila paper. She sat at the large table in her studio while I sat on a kind of shabby armchair she keeps next to the stairs.

Juliana wrote about cribs and infants who writhe in sync with the moon. I wrote about a rat swimming in a sea of ice-cold beer who is happy to be a rat, because even though he lives in the sewer, somehow, down there, the sun still shines through. Other things we wrote that are coming back to me now kind of chaotically: star dust, the energy of conversations, an electric rattle that makes cricket sounds given by a mother (me) to her newborn son, death, the city, the word "Amen."

Now, in my new studio space, I think I'm less alone. Because the gray journal is with me, and the desire to write arises from the love of gifts. A little while ago, I wrote something cheesy but erased it. I wrote how I wanted Juliana and I to keep writing things together on Saturday afternoons even when our hair goes fully gray.

Finally, after so many years of dreaming about this, I have a space that's just for writing. It's a 60-square-foot office near Plaza de Mayo. It's in an old building with spacious halls and a magnificent stairwell with a solid concrete handrail. Or maybe it's stone. I don't know what style it is because I don't really know much about styles, but I'll take a chance and call it neoclassical. The floor is upholstered with ruby-red carpeting with a notable red wine stain on one side, next to a small wooden staircase that leads to a loft area filled with lots of boxes and packages. My boyfriend generously lent me the office, which he has 70 percent ownership of. The other 30 percent belongs to a ridiculously rich woman who uses the space to store her art collection, acquired by and large in the '90s. The sculptures and paintings are lined up in gray boxes or packed up with the kind of bubble wrap that makes you want to pop it bubble by bubble. All of this is to say that this story and all the ones thereafter in the journal will be written while I'm in a room of artwork in a state of rest... or wait...

hibernation. I'm not sure what you call a collection of paintings and sculptures that spend months and then years in boxes where nobody can see them. Can you even call it a "collection?" I'll call it a "hidden collection." The first time I saw them, I felt like I, too, was the owner of a hidden collection of literary works of art, which live in a state of sleep within me. You could say that the writer in me or the literary works on the verge of unfolding from within me (at maximum strength and speed) have been in a state of hibernation within my soul.

Until today. Because from now on, I make a promise to myself and to all my readers, too, that everything, everything, everything I write from today until the day I die will be beautiful and brilliant.

Amalia Ulman (A Happy Week)

Yesterday was the start of a happy week. And if my week was happy, it was thanks to the people I ran into. I'll make a list of each of them as a form of gratitude. I'm not obsessed with lists, but sometimes I need them. Especially lately, when I haven't been able to figure out how to speak about joy. Even if these people never end up reading this text, I still think a piece of my gratitude will touch them anyway. For, as Mario Levrero says, writing about reality means surrendering yourself to the mysterious forces controlling the world.

Friday
Thank you, Sabrina, my Pilates instructor. Feeling my body is a form of happiness. I made it up to that loft with Astroturf for carpet and walls painted a hideous, unfortunate shade of purple, expecting the class to be like all the ones at the other gym I used to go to. A class where, despite having gone for two years straight, I never learned the basic technique of Pilates (or at least nobody ever explained it to me well enough): that all strength must come from your core. It's because it was a cheap gym in an anything-but-glamorous neighborhood like mine, where the clients aren't all that

demanding—me included, clearly. But yesterday, Sabrina explained this technique to me, and I internalized it. While doing my exercises, I realized I felt 20 years old again and that I'd always feel like that, because it was something in my soul, not my body. I also felt like going to the gym would help me write sincere poems that a twenty-year-old would write, like the ones Francisco Garamona writes right on his Facebook, sharing everything he's feeling in the moment.

Thank you to my son, Felix, and his fifth-grade classmate Isabella. I went to pick them up from school to go out for lunch and study chapter three of their natural science textbook before their afternoon test. We studied nutrition, lipids, proteins, and carbohydrates. I learned that a vitamin-B deficiency can cause problems with your circulatory system and that lipids have 9 calories in every 100 grams, whereas carbohydrates only have 4. It was something I never knew. Up until now, I always thought bread made you fatter than olive oil.

Thank you, Lucas, the student in my writing workshop who volunteered to kick off our solos' reading cycle that I came up with to make good use of the office space my boyfriend lent me. The twenty-five-minute show you put together was like a UFO landing in downtown Buenos Aires. You memorized all your poems and recited them using your body in a way that left everybody with their jaws on the floor. You beat your thighs, leapt, prayed on bent knees, and followed the rhythm of the two last raps rapping your knuckles. Your message permeated the air indelibly like ether. Now my office is imbued with those words.

Thank you, Claudio, for lying with me in my dark room and spooning me while I told you everything I learned that afternoon about lipids. You explained how minerals act like an electrical current causing our muscles to move. While you were talking, I asked you how many millions of years those salts (potassium, sodium, calcium) had been on Earth. "Always," you replied. I asked, "Why doesn't anything else make them? They don't come from anywhere? Do they?" And you answered, "They're made in the stars." Even though we hardly have sex anymore, that conversation was better than making love.

Saturday

Thank you, artist from a snobby gallery in La Boca, for making a work of art with red curtains and hundreds of photographs of a pigeon. I felt and also wrote on the last page of the book I had in my purse that, "Love is an experiment." That you can love a human and, also, when everything with other humans is going wrong, you can still love a street pigeon.

Thank you, Julia Roberts, for acting 27 years ago in a movie I never saw when it came out called *Sleeping with the Enemy* about the violence we sometimes face as women. Your movie helped me understand how, for many years, I was the victim of abuse by men and women, too. When you shot your husband three times at the end, killing him, I also understood that the only way to end abuse is to eliminate the source of it. That it's impossible to negotiate with violence.

Sunday

Thank you, woman who works in the corner store across the street from my place. After I bought a loosey, you told me, "Well, it's just one cigarette. You're not so bad. You were a lot worse last year, when you bought 'em three at a time."

Thank you, Nova Radio in Paris, which I was listening to while taking a bath, for playing a song that says, "Everybody must get stoned." And thank you, Bob Dylan, for writing, singing, and recording it in 1968. At first I thought the song was about drugs, but then I realized what it's actually saying is that they will stone us all.

Monday

Thank you, all my Pilates classmates that are my age, because after attentively studying how you do your hair, I decided never to dye my own hair again. I became convinced that having gray hair is better than dying it a fake color, if the price you must pay for coloring it is having straw hair that's some sad, nondescript color—the outcome of successive rounds of supermarket-bought hair dye. I don't want hair like that. I want to age with healthy hair.

Tuesday

Thank you, Gary, for inviting me to host a launch for my book published in Mexico at Ruy's house, which actually isn't so much a house as it is a loft, close to my place. Two days before the event, I went to bed after having a fight with my boyfriend. The air was cool like a solid ice cube. I don't know what substances our neurons emit when people treat each other poorly, but something lingers in the air that carries over to our dreams. I had frightening nightmares from 12 until 3 a.m., when I woke up. In my dream, there were deformed monsters who were demons, faceless demons who were destructive forces. Forces of evil who entered my home and mentally tortured me and my friend, who had the same name as me. The dream seemed so real that I felt like I was trapped in a jail cell with no exit made from energies whose force would never wane. Until I managed to escape and woke up. And right then, I got a WhatsApp message from you, Gary, with the event flyer, which you had just finished designing. There were two monstrous aliens, two alien faces in the foreground lit up by a fluorescent light. Even though I was afraid when I first saw them, then I became calm. Because now the evil forces from my dreams had a face, and I had proof that the dream world and reality aren't as far apart as they seem. It takes a person to separate them after all. It takes a person to separate light from darkness with a conscious act of will. Like lifting a sword of fire in the darkness.

Do It Yourself

I teach a writing workshop every other week on Saturdays at 11 a.m. We do the workshop at another teacher's house. (His name is Santiago Llach.) Twenty years ago, Santiago and I studied at a liberal arts college together. Now, we teach a writing workshop out of his house in downtown Buenos Aires. Even though we never really did much together before, I think we always felt like we shared similar thoughts about writing. Maybe that's why, earlier this year, Santiago wrote me an email asking if I wanted to teach a writing workshop with him. And I said yes. It was simple, because teaching a writing workshop is a simple thing to do. Though, at the same time, I do think it's a totally addictive activity. Everyone all around you, the ways you can look at them and study their gestures, how they become ingrained in your memory. Young people, old people, the things they read. Supposedly, they pay us to say something about what they write. But in reality, if I were rich, *I* would pay *them* to let me listen. Of course, we know everything is backwards from how it should be. Those who work should be rich, and those who are rich should work. The world is like that. Everything that happens carries the mark of its unrealized potential. Those who pay to share their texts ought to charge for doing so, and those of us who charge to listen should have to pay a fortune. I don't care how cheesy it sounds: When they share their stories, when they try to condense their lives into words, when they display their imperfect attempts at writing, they give me something of immeasurable worth. I think it's like being 4 years old again and listening to the stories my godmother used to tell me on the nights when I slept over at her place during summer break. Whenever she reached the end of a book, she would say, "Now I'll make one up for you." And she would begin to narrate her day's events in a mostly realistic way, but always with a twist—some fantastic or surprising element.

Listening to stories. I, for one, could spend my whole life in a reading circle in a Buenos Aires living room listening to stories, directing my attention to attempts to write a poem or a novel. I love failed attempts and those lines of text that come out like a thread weaving the failures. I think of literature as a huge blanket covering an absence. One time when I was 25, a girl gave me a book of poems she made with her home printer as a gift. The cover was a rectangle of pink wool knitted with a garter stitch. She knitted each cover by hand, one at a time, with two needles. The book was titled *Girls*. In one of the poems, a woman said that everything was her mother's fault. In writing workshops, there are no mothers— just words. Words floating around the living room, circulating through the air of a penthouse in the middle of a massive city, a dense metropolis. Really, I should say, "Words forming the ether of a megalopolis." Writing workshops are a city thing. Maybe literature is too? Every day, I dream of spending the day in a bar thinking up stories, ordering coffee among strangers and writing. But I never do it.

There's a guy in our workshop that always reads stories with scenes where he's alone in random bars late at night. He talks to the female bartenders or sees a rock band. Every Saturday, I come really close to telling him that being alone in a bar is, in a way, the essence of literature. But I never actually say it, because at the same time, I think it's a pretty stupid idea.

Today, I left the workshop and went to a Starbucks to get coffee. But first, I passed by a bookstore. I said, "I have 1,300 pesos in my pocket, which I just earned from the workshop. I should invest some of that money into books." And I went straight to the table of new releases and picked up two: *Primary Colors* and *Hallucinations*. I didn't have any points of reference about the authors, but I loved the titles. I let myself get carried away by how their titles sounded. Like when I was 19 and had just moved to this megalopolis and walked into bookstores amazed, purchasing books based off nothing more than my fleeting intuitions, driven by an impulse.

I also bought the book *Hallucinations* because it seemed highly relevant to purchase a book with a title like that after leaving the living room of a house where six people of different ages, genders, and socioeconomic backgrounds attempt to put some fragment of the patchwork of their lives into words. And not only that, but they do it all while also trying to appeal to some concept of beauty. In other words, they perform the aesthetics of words. And beauty could be thought of as a hallucination. Something built by the mind. Or by the collective mind of humanity. (For I'm not the only one who, on some days, believes she's seen beauty come through the door.)

Sometimes I wonder if I'll live to uphold my belief in beauty. I like to think that if I live to uphold that faith, then one day, I, personally, will be more beautiful. Beautiful, albeit elderly. I think that what comes out of a writing workshop is a momentary spiritual fusion. Some people might see something vampire-like in what I've said. And sometimes, when the workshop ends and the students leave to walk home, I truly do feel bloodless.

The whole thing is… Writing is really weird. And hard, too. Picking up a pen and writing about loneliness, for example, about always being alone waiting for the arrival of a great love, which is the theme that almost all the workshop attendees write about (even if they try to disguise it, claiming it's a reflection on society). The truth is there is no place where one is lonelier—and more helpless—than when they write. Whether they're dressed in fine clothes or house rags, whether they're somewhere scenic or awful, it doesn't matter. Married or divorced… Writing is the opposite of peace. Writing is something totally uncomfortable. Because when you write, a vortex opens up in the sky and the voice of an authoritative father screams, "Do it yourself! Do it yourself! Do it yourself!" Do it yourself; nobody will help you. Last Monday, just two students showed up. A girl who lives in New York but is spending a few months in Buenos Aires came in Lycra leggings with a weird pattern, moss green on bright yellow with bits of orange. I couldn't figure out what the pattern was alluding to: psychedelics or ancient Egypt? The poem she brought spoke of how words are like blood in the mouth. She also said that she thinks real literature must scare you. The other boy who came read a text by Marguerite Yourcenar and said something about orphanhood that made me very sad. That orphanhood could exist, even if you had parents. That sometimes you are an orphan even in the most normal of families. He said that he was going to write a novel about this. And he read a text about two people who meet at a gay bathhouse—an asphyxiating locale, according to him—where they'd gone only to hook up.

"Some people spend their whole weekend at the bathhouses," he said. And I became sad, for I started to think that maybe I was a lonely, orphaned person. Maybe I was just teaching a writing workshop so I wouldn't have to be alone. Santiago's living room isn't asphyxiating, and I don't think people come to the workshop just to hook up, at least not consciously so. But if I really think about it, I can't deny that sitting there reading what somebody else has written has a sexual component to it. In a writer's workshop, you get naked. Rather, they get naked, and I watch them. Or they all watch each other, as the sheets they've printed drop and scatter across the floor as they read.

Or maybe they don't get naked. Maybe instead, they hide behind their lies. (Sometimes I seem to forget that literature is all lies, deliria, fictions.) Some Saturdays when I leave the workshop at Santi's house, I walk along Talcahuano or Uruguay Street toward my neighborhood, and it seems like a new, unknown city to me. I feel like I'm walking aimlessly, floating on a cloud. As if I didn't have a body. As if I'd forgotten about hunger and all material aspects of life. As if, thanks to the writing workshop, I could penetrate the heart of literature (which is nothing but a halo of blue or peach light, something like those rings of blue fire near Dracula's castle when Keanu Reeves speeds by in a carriage in the Francis Ford Coppola movie.)

What Is a Poem?

I live in Buenos Aires, a city where everyone I know is doing something. Everyone has some kind of project going on, but... Could anybody be writing a poem at this very moment? Sometimes, I try to imagine how many people at this exact moment could be doing the exact same thing as me... (Although it turned out otherwise, this story was meant to be a poem.)

First, I go over all the people I know who could be writing a poem in my head. Jaqueline, Martina, Pablo, Francisco, Luz, Rodrigo, Candela, Claudio... people who logically might be doing it because it's what they do for a living. Or better put, it's their main hobby, 'cause who really devotes themselves fully to poetry? *Devoting* oneself, with a verb like that, to poetry seems like hell or an insult. Hell in the sense of a hellish punishment, the kind with no end. Because a poem never ends. That's the problem. It can always be better, or even worse. It will always, always, always be bad. There is no way—even if you deconstruct it and put it back together again, over and over like a puzzle—for a poem to be perfect. And an insult because declaring that you're devoted to poetry would be offensive to the great poets, like Enrique Lihn, whom I only can read and worship closing my eyes and hearing their voices on YouTube. Yesterday, I listened to Enrique Lihn read a poem about laziness, and it felt good. Because I was so tired of my never-ending cleaning routine in my house, which anyway always stays unorganized and dirty. (Because a house is just like a poem: It's never done being organized and cleaned.) Still, thinking about the beauty of laziness that Enrique Lihn mentioned gave me relief. A laziness that, nevertheless, is actually quite hard for me to achieve in real life because I am a mother. I must always take care of the house and my son. What he eats, his clothes, making sure he's having fun, whether or not he read a book... Even though laziness hasn't been a part of my own life story, I can still accomplish laziness as a daydream... or a platonic idea. In Santiago, a young publisher told me that Enrique Lihn didn't take care of his children, but I don't care. I don't care that he was a man and had the structural privileges all men have. I won't hate him for that. His imperfect poet's voice makes me happy on this ordinary day's twilight.

Anyway, as I was saying, the possibility of enjoying laziness, even if it's just for a brief few hours, gave me the idea of writing a contemporary poem (because a 20th-century poem, like the one Enrique Lihn wrote, already seems impossible to write in 2017). My thought was: I'm going to send the following question to everybody that I think might be writing a poem at this exact moment via WhatsApp:

"Hi, I was wondering what a poem is for you... I'd appreciate it if you could define it in just a few words."

A few hours went by with no response, even though WhatsApp told me that almost everybody I sent the message to—about ten friends—had read it. I was sitting on my turquoise faux-leather chair as the afternoon passed, with my phone in hand and gaze locked on the small garden on the other side of my living room's sliding glass doors. And nobody answered. I rested my Samsung Galaxy Lite, with a cracked cover, against my forehead for a long time, then on my stomach, and finally on my heart, in hopes that this arbitrary and kind of ritual gesture would telepathically unleash the literary desire to answer me on my message's recipients.

Eventually, it was 12 a.m., and there I was. I hadn't eaten. Didn't watch the news. Hadn't showered. I'd done nothing... My son ate three apples we had in the fridge and went to bed.

Around 2 a.m., I heard the sound of my phone telling me I had a new message, but multiplied by 10-to-20 percent. It was a waterfall of dings! A symphony! A rave! It was like suddenly all of my 21st-century poet friends had decided to define poetry at the same time—2 a.m. My heart leapt.

These are some of the messages I transcribed:

I don't know what a poem is, but the kitchen table covered in the breadcrumbs leftover from breakfast feels like the perfect place to write a poem. A poem is a house, a castle, a fountain, blood. Though, in the shower, I didn't think a poem was any of those things, but actually a piece of music. A poem is a poodle trapped in an enormous, oversized red Jell-O cube. A poem is an old heated pool about to crack. A poem is eating dinner amidst the uncombed, furious heads of African lilies. A poem is walking around the house naked with a black silk belt tied around your waist. The part of your yard where two different species of grass overlap and blend: sedges and carpet grass. A poem is when I want to learn to love. A poem is the never-ending addiction to a poem.

The list goes on, but I'm getting tired. I'll wrap it up tomorrow.

The Flawed Concept of Coupledom

From one moment to the next, my ideas changed completely. I can't remember exactly how it happened, but I do vaguely remember that less than thirty minutes ago, I was trying to come up with a title and concept for a story that sounded brilliant. But now I can't remember its exact formulation. I know it was some expression about couples. Now I'm calling it "The Flawed Concept of Coupledom," but those weren't the exact words. It was something far more interesting, synthetic, and deeper than this title. And while I know how the phrase felt, I can't remember what "aesthetic" sensation it produced.

It can be quite frustrating.

Be as it may, what surprises me isn't that I forgot the expression. I've already accepted that forgetfulness is a key part of writing, of literature. For me, what I publish and sell (which, as an aside, I do very little of) aren't books but rather all my small ideas—whether brilliant or moronic, but either way, surprising and liberating (at the time)...or libertarian— I have throughout the day that don't make it to the page. Generally, these ideas turn into titles. And what beautiful titles they are! (Which isn't to say they are slogans.) Luxurious titles rich with meaning that will never serve any purpose, because the text that should follow them never gets written. I'd love to do a gallery exhibit of titles. I envision walking into a large gallery illuminated by a bright blue light, and there, my titles are all on display. Not on the walls, because they wouldn't exactly be paintings. What I'm picturing is a mental gallery whose address and coordinates I, and only I, have. To get to my showing of titles, I need only lie down in my bed with turquoise sheets and close my eyes… Each title leads to another—sometimes related, sometimes not—like a necklace of fake beads made in a frenzy. Although the way I dream them, they're one great whole. Suddenly, the blue gallery becomes ectoplasm, and the titles and my arteries are one and the same, a single unit. After "The Flawed Concept of Coupledom" comes another title: "The Creator and the Fires of Artifice." Each title gives way to a special moment in my life where my mind tries to understand everything it sees or experiences. And then there is a great stretch of white walls, because aphasia is also a part of this gallery. That space where poetry ends and life is but a golden corner.

I don't know why I thought that the concept of coupledom was bad. Unfortunately, I can't remember all the feelings and sensations that brought me to think so anymore. Because now I'm happy and feel blessed since you gave me a blue, British hat while walking along Paseo Ahumada, and it was a lucky day. That's the next title I'll add: "A Lucky Day." Something like that to try and trap the luck before it fades away. I think the title about the flawed concept of coupledom is from November, and things have changed since then. Now it's January, and coupledom is perfect. I want it on the record here. Each night, we watch a movie on Netflix. And each morning, we have coffee at Harvard, a café-bar at the corner of Alberti and Hipólito Irigoyen Street. Life is simple, and titles don't come to me like they did before. Suddenly, I realize that the day has gone by, and I haven't thought of a single one. My mind's gallery begins to clear out, and reality bursts in like an onslaught of occurrences that need not be named. Could this be happiness? And if so, is happiness the opposite of writing? I move forward on the blank page, and a minor angst settles on my shoulders. It's like an assault. As if some strange animal had entered my room, an animal I've never seen before. Why can't writing and happiness be simultaneous? The animal says I must light a cigarette and write a new title: "Ballad of a Woman Who Smokes." It commands me to go buy three looseys from the corner store across the street. The animal, which could be an alien visiting from another universe to infect me, reminds me that I used to write to earn luck, and now that I've got it, it doesn't make sense to keep stockpiling phrases on paper.

But in the afternoon, I get dressed to go to work. I teach for a living, and I have to run a workshop for kids at the Modern Art Museum of Buenos Aires. I wear a t-shirt with a print of bold colors—a burst of vibrancy. I feel like it's a good way to keep the participants' attention. I was mulling over and preparing the workshop for two months with a girl from the museum. The kids will work in the gallery, writing anything they want on a wooden board. I'll tell them they must ask the paintings questions and then answer them, as if they themselves were the works and could talk. In the middle of the gallery, there is a polished metal sculpture. Maybe it's steel. It's a mass with irregular edges. It could be a piece of scrap metal from a spaceship or a crumbled piece of paper. A 12-year-old boy asks, "In the world you come from, how big are you and what are you? Are you a small part of something much bigger or are you something huge in a world of tiny, negligible things?"

The other participants and I stare it at him entranced. We all think it's a brilliant question. And what's more, we love his use of the word "negligible." If everything in the world can be a part of something else we don't know, then it's likely that my mental gallery of titles—an idea that gives me comfort and anxiety at the same time—has another meaning aside from the one I've given it. If things are like that, as Nehuel says, then certainly everything I write and everything that comes to me has nothing to do with me or my life story or happiness or coupledom or the blue hat or luck… They must be mere fragments of something much bigger or smaller that exists in another dimension.

Freestyle Rap

Today is a beautiful, perfect fall day. I'm watching the philodendron leaves in my garden. Philodendrons have always made me feel like I live in a jungle, despite being in a pretty central urban neighborhood full of cars and smog. I hear the sound of my washing machine. The last ray of afternoon sunlight falls at an angle across my unmade bed, giving the sheets a golden hue and make me ask: Is it powdered gold? Is this powdered gold? Is light just powdered stars? Sometimes, when silence grows thick, I say: Now. Now! It's time to write a book. But quickly, another sensation takes over, and I feel like it's too late. The year is 2047. I was born in 1973. I'm 73 now. I started teaching writing workshops in 2004, when I was 31. That is to say I've spent forty-three years doing this. It's impossible for me to tabulate how many bodies have passed through my living room (most were women's), the same eternal living room with ceramic terracotta floors that, on each of those workshop Fridays, I lovingly cleaned with lavender- or ocean breeze–scented floor cleaner to welcome my guests in a completely clean home. I always felt it was important for the house to be impeccable whenever workshop participants came to sit in my living room and read me poems and stories or chapters of the novels they were working on. It was a key part of the ritual, because from my perspective, more so than being a class, the workshop was a ceremony. If the house wasn't in perfect order, the exchange didn't work, the poems they'd read wouldn't sound good to me, their plots would be a failure and bore everyone in attendance... Now that I think about it, all these superstitions built on the belief that my actions could influence aspiring poets and novelists must have been nothing more than an illusion arising from my fear of writing a novel, a hallucination. Instead of writing a novel myself, I would clean the house so that others could do so. And with a mysterious bow, I would tie up the house with words. Or, once the workshops wrapped up and the sun went down, I'd go with the students on the bus to readings in basements where just the girls—with their countless different poses—would read. Girls with ribbons in their hair and acid-washed jeans who avoided, just as I did, dealing with text and writing. I've never talked about this in the workshop. In reality, I've never talked about it with anybody. But it's a topic that constantly occupies my mind: the difference between poses and writing.

Now that the years have passed, I'm realizing that writing—what is called writing—I've never written it. In turn, what I've done is a perfect, beautiful pose. ("Strike a pose," as Madonna said.) Writing never came to me in the form of essence or a spark; I've never felt the electricity of the letters spilling from my veins onto the paper, lighting it ablaze. It's sad, because it's too late. I've never published a novel, save for this brief survey of my shortcomings, which is nothing more than a humble attempt at an excuse or an entryway to another dimension.

My whole life I believed that a book could be a springboard to another dimension. And if I managed to create a world wrapped up in blankets of words, I could be somebody else. And my mind would work like a robot. Or a parrot. Or, upon seeing myself in the mirror, I would feel like a fleshy, velvety flower. But instead of writing a novel, I started to teach a writing workshop. (Of course, it was also a means of getting by.)

The meetings had two distinct parts to them. During the first half, students had to discuss whatever reading I had assigned them, by writers like Alejandra Pizarnik, Thomas Pynchon, or Héctor Viel Temperley, just to name a few. In the second half, they had to bring a poem they wrote following some instruction or rule I had come up with. One day I told them, "When you get home, open the door and close your eyes. Walk blindly until you run into something, and then write a poem dedicated to whatever object you ran into. For example, if you run into the edge of a cupboard and start bleeding, let the blood stain the paper you write on. Don't go to the hospital; don't clean the cut. Write a poem." Another time I instructed them, "Grab a hundred-peso bill from your pocket and go to the first bookstore you find and buy any old book. Then go home and take it out of the bag, but don't read it. Tonight, when you go to sleep, put it under your pillow and caress it. The next day, contemplate it while you eat breakfast, and then re-write it on yellow sheets of paper with a blue pen." Sometimes, I asked them to write a poem while riding a bike and memorize it. To never write it on paper, but spend the whole week memorizing it until the day they'd reach my living room and recite it out loud. Or to write their poem while watching a movie at the theater. Or buying something at the supermarket. The key was to memorize it. To write it in their head. For their poem to be a song and never be written down.

Like I said, the writing workshop was a way to earn a living. It gave me income based on the works of dead people who could never file a legal claim against me for using their creations. Dead. Or alive, but in a far-away country where they would never find out. Poets we invoked at each session. (And why pretend it isn't true? A writer's workshop is a séance too, after all.) Though I ought to note that, over the decades, I've also assigned many contemporary Argentine authors, my travel companions, as reading. And some of them have even come to the workshop. Once, in 2013, Ezequiel Alemián, a writer I've known since I was 25, mistreated me in front of my students, and I stopped speaking to him. I'm not sure why I'm telling you this, actually. It doesn't make any sense. Whatever... So much time has passed. Who cares whom I fought or made up with? Fight or no fight—I still never wrote my novel.

And this short draft of a text simply serves to bear witness that I'm now 73 years old, and the decades have passed without me ever having sat down and said, "Now! Now is the time to write."

And where, for instance, are the poems written by the workshop students from winter 2014? Did they wind up in an anthology or published online? What ever happened to Luisina Gentile, who was finishing up her degree in sociology, but hated the rational paradigm of human science and wanted a change of scene? And to meet girls, because she liked women, and according to Luisina, Buenos Aires doesn't have the best scene for gay women (for the men, sure, but for lesbians, not so much). She must be 50 or so now. Did she end up in France? Berlin? New York? Like she always dreamt of? She also said she wanted to get a scholarship so she could attend college. Or to go somewhere without any money and try her luck. To rap freestyle—her favorite genre of music. (Did she end up having any kids? Has she written any books?) One cold Friday in mid-May, I gave her workshop an assignment to quote Catullus. The next week, Luisina brought this short poem:

(punk rock)

Todo esto lo invento,	*I'm making all this up,*
como vos	*Yeah, I'm just like you,*
Catulo	*Catullus,*
que seguro lo habrás hecho	*I bet that's what you did*
Vos te la bancás y se te nota	*You put up with a lot, I see it*
Yo no tanto pero no importa	*Not like me, I just don't need it*
También quiero decir	*I tell 'em all to kiss my ass*
que me la chupen	*And I wish they'd say it back*
Incluso quiero que	*But meeting girls isn't easy.*
alguien me diga que se la chupe	*No, it isn't. Really!*
Pero conocer chicas no es fácil	
Posta. Nada fácil.	

Hoy después del psiquiatra en Recoleta	*Today, I saw my therapist in Recoleta*
voy al taller de Cecilia en Balvanera	*I've got Cecilia's workshop in Balvanera*
Después quizás salgo un poco	*Maybe later, I'll go out a bit*
Para eso, te confieso.	*That's mostly why I'm saying this*
Después de vos, Catulo (54 a.c) vino Cristo	*After you, Catullus (54 BC) came Jesus*
No te imaginás cuantas éticas que afanaron con esa historia, los hijos de puta	*You won't believe all the morality Assholes made up from that whole story*
En parte también es por eso que es tan difícil conocer chicas, Catulito…	*And that, Catullus, is another reason why It's so hard to find women in my life…*

When she finished reading, the other students clapped. I smiled and said I was touched that she put my name in her writing. It's true. There are millions of Cecilias in literature… ok, maybe hundreds. But the phrase "Cecilia's workshop in Balvanera" must only exist in that poem. It was like a lullaby or a powerful drug—something intoxicating that filled me with vanity and pride.

I don't care if anybody calls me a narcissist. I think that simple phrase—written in a poem lost on a sheet of paper in 2014, a poem of which perhaps just five or six copies were made—is now, at this precise moment, the Literature (with a capital "L") that comes to mind while gazing at my beautiful garden.

And although I never wrote a novel, my name was in a line of a poem by a stunning girl who always said she wanted to do freestyle rap. And is there anything more poetic than freestyle rap?

Two Stories about Downtown Buenos Aires

I definitely don't want to be a professional writer—that I know! But this afternoon, with the twenty-five minutes left before I have to go back to work, I'd like to force myself to write a story about downtown Buenos Aires, because it's been two years since I've written a story, and today it occurred to me to write one. If I ever publish another book, there will be a blank page that says: *Two Stories about Downtown Buenos Aires.*

I know that I'll be happy with a title like that.

I don't know if my readers will be too, but I will, because downtown Buenos Aires is an important place in my life.

Yet at the same time, I can't figure out it's a place that brings up good memories or bad ones. I mean, I don't know if it's safe... or full of enemies... or just problematic. But whatever... that's the ambiguity here. The generalized ambiguity that guides my existence. Though you could call it a toy ambiguity, a plastic one. First of all, and for now, let's say downtown is an ambiguous place, because at the moment, it has no defined or clear personality. That's because downtown Buenos Aires is a point of transit, a neighborhood of offices and financial transactions, just a casual backdrop for the circulation of money. And money is an ambiguous force, an ambivalent fluid that can go anywhere, can end up in anything or at any event.

Now, why is downtown such a problematic place in my life? Because my boyfriend, the love of my life, my Lover (with a capital "L" now, for it is a timeless love) left me two years ago to come live in this neighborhood. And here, in one of these bland bars that all look the same, he met a girl from abroad and also a dealer, and my boyfriend became a heroin addict.

Now that so much time has passed, whenever I have the chance, I walk around downtown in a kind of eternal state of mourning, waiting for the moment I come across my ex holding hands with his new girlfriend, speaking English, on one of the pedestrian streets or sitting together in some coffee shop. Or just snorting heroin in a bathroom.

What he takes isn't exactly heroin, at least not the heroin of the '90s that Kurt Cobain took, the kind you inject straight into your bloodstream. It's a pill, a synthetic opioid that you grind up and snort. (He told me all about his new addiction in an email, the only way we've stayed in touch, infrequent as it is.)

Sometimes I spend hours in bed staring at the ceiling, imagining myself flying through the sky, seeing all the houses and apartments from above with a special kind of vision that can see through rooftops. And then I see him, asleep with his new girlfriend, curled up naked in the fetal position. And I can also see through all the furniture, and I see the pills he snorts. They're small, in his nightstand drawer. I don't know what color those little pills are, so I start making up colors.

They must be light blue or orange or maybe pink, I wonder. I don't think they would be any other color.

I go to the Bidou, the Saint Moritz, the London, all the café-bars downtown. And I concentrate. I close my eyes and visualize him so that he'll finally manifest once and for all… but he never shows up. He's never anywhere to be found. Or maybe he is, but only in my memories. And I never get away from his influence. And when I wander aimlessly through the streets of that part of the city, I feel his invisible care form a huge magnetic field of heat… a kind of spaceship or invisible bubble that drags me toward a state of ambiguity. And ambiguity is literature.

David Bowie died the other day, and they were playing his music everywhere. They kept putting on that song called "Major Tom" where he talks about an astronaut. Listening to it, I felt like I, too, was an astronaut. I envisioned my ex as Earth, and what I call literature my spaceship, the tin can in which I drifted, and we lost touch forever. Because when he abandoned me so cruelly, from one day to the next, it couldn't just have been for me to suffer. The fact that he is distant and loves me like a ghost is what allows me to write. Because I am an abandoned woman, *I can write*. I can say "I" a million times. And by saying "me me me," I can also say that a woman who is loved from a close proximity instead of from afar cannot write. (This idea just came to me, and I can't really defend it. But I'm still committing it into writing here, as if it were a casual note. I know that within an hour, I'll probably reconsider, and my idea won't seem true anymore, as it's nothing more than a byproduct of pain.)

In any case, yesterday was the first day of spring. At 3:30, after crying for two hours in my beautiful bed, I felt an impulse to take the subway to Peru Street and sit on the terrace at the London Café. It was a gorgeous day. Sitting there calmly, I saw endless people hustling and bustling along Peru Street. They were all in such a rush, while I remained still, immobile. I tried staying as still as possible so I could feel their velocity.

I wrote my first story about downtown Buenos Aires in Bidou Bar, across the street from the Stock Exchange, back when my boyfriend had already met the other woman but hadn't told me about her yet. I reread that story recently, and my blood ran cold as it made me think of the divinatory power of writing: its oracular power.

Or whatever you want to call it.

I'm referring to that power that (what I call) literature has: its power to illuminate something in process that has yet to be formulated with words. The story was simple, almost an outline. It was about a housewife walking around downtown with one of those wheeled backpacks (like the ones for school), who sits in a café across from the Stock Exchange and starts writing. She believed translation could breathe new life into her existence... To be honest, my story's plot doesn't exactly match the real events that happened to me, which were like a whirlwind, a total hurricane. From one day to the next, my boyfriend became an opioid addict and ran off with an American girl. But my story did have the United States in it. And it also had translation in it. (Obviously, the basis of my ex's relationship with the American girl is some kind of translation.) And that short story whose plot I came up with also had the experience of escaping time in it, which is what my boyfriend must feel every time he gets high and also what I'm feeling now.

You can escape time through joy or through pain: The housewife in my story escaped time through the joy of translation, and I did it through the pain of disappointment.

All of this is to say that downtown Buenos Aires is a place of divination. Which is similar to distraction. And distraction is central to literature. But those thoughts will end up in another story. For now, let's continue with what's happening here and now on this fantastic spring afternoon:

I've decided to hold back my tears for the moment, take out my notebook, and transcribe the conversation I can overhear from the next table over. The speakers are two gay men who seem to be on a first date. They mention something about the app they met on and the name of some mutual contact they both vaguely know. Then they jump quickly to a topic that surprises me: They start talking blood. I find it to be an unusual topic for a first date, but who knows, maybe the world is different and blood is a completely casual topic today. I know that being in love with a ghost has taken me completely out of time, and I guess it's possible the world is changing too quickly for me to notice while I'm so out of touch with things. I keep writing what I overheard.

The heftier guy says he has an illness (I can't make out the name) that causes intense symptoms: exhaustion, flu, and he gets sick a lot, basically all the time. He emphasizes the flu and points out his skin, which is full of pockmarks from his illness.

Still, he maintains a healthy lifestyle: exercises a lot, and doesn't smoke or drink. The breeze blows a little stronger, and I miss something he says. I can't make out exactly what illness afflicts him, but now he's talking about how when he was 17, he was in a hospital on Mitre Street where a doctor offered to perform a blood transfusion for him, but he refused because he had heard there was a risk of organ damage. Later, the other guy started telling his own story: how when he was born, he spent six months in the NICU with some rare disease. (Again, the wind carried its name away from me.) Then, a heroic doctor, the best doctor in (I think he said) Quilmes (or maybe it was Ituzaingó) speaks with his parents and says it to them straight: "Your preemie's only hope is a total blood transfusion. But it can't be done here in Argentina. You'll have to take him to Japan. I have all the right contacts there." And just like that, they went to Japan, did the transfusion, and came back. And now he is alive and well.

Pain is so strange, I think. Illnesses are so strange. And then, all of a sudden, something brilliant happens. Again, the downtown air brings illumination, and I restore the feeling within me that literature is the oracle of all oracles. As if every word I write forms a chain of some enduring material, whose links are small premonitions that turn out to be true. And then, it seemed like it truly had been worth it to take out my notebook and write, for no good reason, everything I heard around me. Overhearing those men talk about their illnesses made me think of my own. And I'm having a realization that I, too, suffer from an illness. My illness is common and ordinary... and god, how haven't I ever realized this before?!

What I have isn't metaphysical or astral or even literary. It's a much more common feeling called nostalgia. Now I know that's what I'm feeling. My tears, my yearning, and my pride in writing about abandonment and loneliness—it all amounts to nothing. And these three pages don't mean anything either. Just like downtown, which also means nothing. And something much more important: I'll never be a writer.

After realizing that, I feel light. I pay for my coffee, close my journal, and go walking, content, along Avenida de Mayo.

Untitled

It's splendid to waste money when you earn it with such ease. As if it were light, clean, and you were doing something good for humanity, and the twenty dollars coming out of your wallet will stimulate hundreds of industries. As of now, that green scarf with gold threads is on its way from the store to your house. Money makes things magically move around the city. Memories are illusions. Objects are the only things that stay with us over the years, times, and money. When you die, it'll happen in your bed, surrounded by beautiful, meaningful possessions: clothes made by talented designers or photography books with heavy pages. Expensive clothes are the only thing that does the body good. Books by young German poets are beautiful and cost money. Beachwood rocking chairs are beautiful and cost money. Crystal wine glasses, silver-plated rings, champagne. Oh, it's like the air in the Alps is made of champagne! Up here, nobody should work; they should just spend money. Oh, Alpine dollars! If they took all the money out of the Swiss banks, they could make mountains of Swiss francs.

I'd love to have a room full of euros, floor to ceiling, to go in during the early morning hours when everything is still dark and step on them. I'd grab fistfuls without even checking how much and stuff them in my guests' pockets. I'd sleep on the euros like hay in a stable. I'd be protected by the European Union and its monuments.

Little Joy (Temporary Autonomous Zone)

Translation is the closest thing there is to travel. On the page before my eyes is written the name of a bar in Los Angeles (one that must not be there anymore) called Little Joy. The text is about 2005. In it, Antonio Vera, a Mexican guy who studied film in San Diego with the money he got from an American who hit him while driving drunk in a border town, meets some interesting artists. Although he soon starts to feel strange about being in the States. They were building a wall along the border, and there was tension everywhere, the text says in one passage.

It is 11:30 a.m., and I am translating in the small room next to my kitchen, where I always work. The air reeks of tobacco and there is very little light in here (the sun never shines), but I feel immense joy over having stumbled on the name of that bar. As soon as I finish the words, I immediately start thinking of this place that isn't exactly a bar, but somewhere where people go to drink alcohol anyway (sometimes, a lot of it, and they also take other substances too). I've met many interesting people there.

I think about how lucky I am that they asked me to translate this book, because if I hadn't come across the name of this bar, I never would have felt inspired to write about that place I go to every Wednesday night, which I think is the best place on Earth.

The best place on Earth is this antique shop in Villa Crespo. You can go any time of day. The owner, Brunildo, is always sitting in the back room (the store has two rooms) smoking Virginia Slims—the Superslims variety, which only has half the tobacco and nicotine as every other brand of cigarette. Also, Brunildo always wears Hawaiian shirts with bold colors, a showy contrast to the faded colors of the mahogany and chestnut beds and dining room sets.

But he doesn't sell just furniture. Piled up and forming pillars between the faded, dusty sofas and the coffee tables with their heavy iron fittings, there are thousands upon thousands of books—those things that have fallen almost completely out of use in today's world. Brunildo loves books above everything else, and a lot of the people who meet up at Little Joy every Wednesday night go just for that: to be close to books, and drink and take drugs surrounded by them. Could they be under the illusion that physical proximity to novels and poetry grants them instant access to other worlds without having to waste time opening the books up and reading them? (Oh, the dream of reaching another world! At the end of the day, everyone—I included—dreams of that.) Maybe they bring the books home and read them there, while here they just caress them, as I've seen so many patrons do.

One Wednesday (I don't really know why, I think I had gone somewhere to do some bureaucratic formality), I was close to Little Joy and decided to go spend some time there a little earlier than I usually go. The store was closed. A heavy metal gate covered the window display. I banged on the gate several times, but nobody answered. Then I stood up on my tippy toes and pressed my face against the only opening I could find. A hard, gray sheet kept me from happiness. Bizarrely, the gate had a hole just under an inch in diameter in its farthest upper-left-most corner, as though somebody had pierced it with a bullet (the hole was just that size). On the other side, Brunildo was there on the ground hugging an old book. I couldn't make out the title, but I could see that the cover was all black, a dark black. And Brunildo was crying uncontrollably. Whenever there were no cars in the street, you could just make out his desperate crying through the metal gate. It occurred to me that I had never seen anybody do something like that with a book. Brunildo was cradling it like a baby or a girlfriend, and talking to it, opening up to random pages and whispering to the book through his sobs.

The whole scene affected me. I backed away quickly from that window in the gate and pretended I hadn't seen anything at all. I closed my eyes and set off walking to the nearest subway station. I ran down the stairs, almost sprinting into Malabia Station. I went back home until 11, when we all usually go to the store. I'd like to just clarify that out of our whole group, I'm the only one who doesn't take drugs. Well, maybe I do, but only through osmosis. I am like a vampire of the altered states of everyone else around me. They all take weird drugs I've never even heard of, but because I'm a bit cowardly and have a deep-rooted fear of being out of control, I choose to stay at the margins. I sit there on some beat-up couch and just take it all in. The girls dance reggaeton and run around the store, crazed. Okay, fine, that only happened once. In Little Joy, nothing ever happens twice. Though the men do always act the same way when they're on drugs: They take out toy guns and start shooting at the piles of books.

It's 2017, and people do weird things. Especially ever since the aliens arrived a few months ago, and all of Western culture and Eastern culture and the culture of indigenous peoples, popular culture, high culture, really any type of culture that ever existed on Earth became passé for all of humanity. The arts, literature, and music stopped making sense, as did the State, the family unit, and politics. People did what they had to in order to stay alive. I did what I had to in order to stay alive, including going every Wednesday to Little Joy—my own temporary autonomous zone. This is what I made when the world started over from ground zero. Even though I don't fully understand what I'm doing here, this small antique shop is my only little joy.

In the early '90s, some American theorists (America—where the aliens chose to settle because the Americans' football stadiums work better than any other kind of sports venue for landing their ships) came up with the idea of the TAZ, a temporary autonomous zone. They thought of it as a temporary escape from the power of the State. I don't think the theorists ever thought that so soon, everyone would stop caring about their Earthly anarchism. It's not like the aliens are bad people or want to conquer us, but the culture shock has been so massive that humanity's minds have been in a total haze. Unable to understand anything. Utterly confused, with no idea whatsoever how to act or think. That's why in Little Joy, nobody reads books anymore. They just shoot them and use them to build endless piles that reach the ceiling.

Brunildo, who was into tarot and a clairvoyant before the aliens arrived, knew they were coming months ahead of time. I remember him telling everybody in our poetry readings and art show openings. But nobody took him seriously. Is that why he spent the afternoon sobbing while hugging a book? Maybe, in his mind's confusion, he holds a few memories of when he was the best poet in Buenos Aires. Of course, he is the one who prepares the toy guns for shooting books. But latent somewhere in his conscience, this must be weighing on him.

Dreams Can't Be Copyrighted

It would be so easy to convince people of my vision. All I'd need to do is lead strategically planned tours around the city, like bring everybody first to a clearance at Zara, where screaming, packed crowds would be frantically sorting through unsightly pressed-wood cubes filled with hundreds of poor sweaters made in Indonesia or Brazil. To clarify, I'd take them without any money, so their only option would be to suffer before this disturbing scene of frenzied consumption at the hands of unsatisfied citizens—their peers. When their shock hits peak revulsion, we'd leave and I'd take them to the nearest art gallery. They'd feel such a positive change that they'd all end up joining my party, of which I am the candidate for something. But I'll never really be a candidate for anything. For my agenda is secret, unique, and personal. And anything personal can't be political. In reality, it's the opposite. Anything personal is, in fact, the antidote to society, and I hate society. But I have no option other than to live in one, so I've invented a nonconformist ritual for myself that works as a radicalization machine. It's like this: Whenever I go out, I only go to cultural centers, foundations, and galleries. Spaces designed for displaying art are ample, well lit, and most important, void of people. In

Buenos Aires, there are at least a hundred art galleries of every style, but I always go to the same three or four "hip" ones where the young artists show their work. I don't have anything against older artists, but for me, the only true artists are the young ones, and I don't think that needs a lot of justification. I feel that young artists continue aspiring to be a total human being, and I believe them. And they pass their faith on to me. Wouldn't it be great if all of Earth's inhabitants died, and all that was left were just the artists and I? Their works of art thrill me. I don't care if the execution is only so-so, and I don't care if they're genius or subpar—all that matters is that they exist.

By following my program, staring each day for hours at all kinds of art, entering as many art galleries as I can and avoiding all other derivatives of society, when I close my eyes at night I can envision the entire world reformed by young artists. (Tree trunks growing cushions instead of branches, walls covered in 200 photos taken in 200 minutes at a singular point in space, basketballs split in half with broken encyclopedias inside, paper castles lit on fire, oceans of clay, teddy bears with children's bodies, lighter bicycles for carrying laptop cases, blue satin-coated cables, pianos resting on cushions, women angrily throwing a TV set five times in a row, black-and-white remakes of that Linda Blair movie, and giant books full of text messages.) And I love living like this. I don't need anything else. I don't need to buy things or take drugs or contaminate the planet using Walkmans with batteries or vote for a president who wants to reform the country or stand out from the rest of society. I couldn't care less about the minimum wage. Contemplating art ends all class distinctions and personal insecurities. Further, spectators are as much a part of the work itself as the artists. At least I read that in a British sociology magazine, and I think it's very true and very uplifting. It's far more important being part of a work of art than being part of a society, because works of art are made of dreams, and dreams can't be copyrighted.

A Perfect Day

Any writing that doesn't move toward love will crash against a wall or something else hard, like that one time a train coming into Once Station didn't brake. It's Sunday afternoon, and I'm remembering a perfect day. All of my stories are about thinking or remembering, though I was on the verge of writing a story about killing. That was inspired by a beautiful ceramic sculpture my eight-year-old son made: four knives sticking out of a coarse surface, with moss-green enamel. Each knife is a different size, all gray, and laid out from largest to smallest. However, this isn't the time to talk about knives; it's the time to talk about a perfect day...

January 20, 2016, was a perfect day. A scorching hot day in Santiago, Chile. I arrived in that city hand-in-hand with my son, who was visiting his Chilean father, after crossing the mountains on a bus and waiting five hours at customs. Hordes of Argentines—yes, "hordes" is the most accurate term here—waiting for their chance to enter our neighboring country, spurred on by the hope of finding cheap goods on the other side of the Andes. All thanks to the infamous exchange rate. As if the Argentine peso had ceased to exist. As if it were just a ghostly figure dancing around the American dollar. And it doesn't exist; it's just a weak abstraction floating around a more powerful one, a fistful of dry leaves.

The outgoing president wouldn't let us buy dollars. They needed them for state industries. The incoming president deregulated the exchange of foreign currencies. According to his campaign, his platform was pro-commerce and pro-freedom. Commerce and freedom. It's only been a month since Argentines could start buying dollars the official way again, and already they flock in hordes across the border to buy clothes and computers imported from Asia... Clothes and computers: the two things defining my life. My computer, because it's where I write and I write for a living. (I'm a woman who writes for a living.) And clothes, because they're the most accessible resource I have to make myself a woman so I can be a woman who writes.

On Wednesday, January 20, 2016, I met up with Gary and Eugenia to go shopping at the Costanera Center Mall. A friend of Gary told him that from his building's balcony, the Costanera Center Mall looks like a lit cigarette. There, you can find all the brands we don't have in Argentina because of Néstor and Cristina Kirchner's high duties on textile goods. They have H&M, Forever 21, Topshop, Banana Republic, the Gap... All brands that are almost certainly unfashionable in Europe, but cause a furor in this part of the world. One of the main attractions of the shopping mall is a waterfall that displays images and text amidst the free-falling drops of water. It's twenty-six feet wide and forty feet tall, designed and built by the German company OASE, according to Wikipedia. On Wikipedia, you can find the history of every

Chilean evil. I don't know why I decided to Google this, nor why I'm transcribing it here. Maybe because it caught my attention that the company behind the Costanera Center Mall's branding mentions the waterfall as the mall's main attraction. Or maybe because, despite having spent six hours in that mall, I never saw the images or words supposedly made by those free-falling drops of water. I don't think anybody has seen them, because they're just accessories to the ecstatic experience of shopping. Or perhaps a child has seen them. It could be. When I read about the waterfall, I immediately thought about contemporary art: senseless words and images flowing in free fall to inspire transactions in a market. On Wikipedia, I also found the history of the first Latin American mall, which opened in Chile under Augusto Pinochet's government: "The Parque Arauco Mall opened to the public on April 2, 1982, with an opening ceremony the following day led by commander-in-chief of the Chilean Navy and member of the Chilean military junta, José Toribio Merino." That same date, April 2, in Argentina, the Falklands War began. Could you say, then, that on April 2, 1982, two wars began in the Southern Cone? Well, in reality, the two wars were one and the same, but that would take a lot of effort to explain. I'll just say that a single war moves articles of clothing, arms, and works of art around the world.

To be honest, it doesn't matter where malls come from (or where they go). What matters is that they exist, like cigarettes that are always lit. Or giant fridges, like on that suffocatingly hot day in early 2016. It was the hottest day of the year, and there is almost nowhere with air conditioning in Santiago.

Electricity is expensive in Chile, and only huge companies like the Costanera Center Mall can afford AC. I went there on the subway, by myself, reflecting on my life (which is what I always do when I'm traveling alone on public transportation). My son was with his father's family. And Fabio, who had been my partner for seven years and always came with me when I visited Chile, had left me ten months prior for an American girl. Samantha, a rich girl from California. She came to Buenos Aires to get away from her authoritarian father—another war, it would seem. Fabio met her in one of those tourist-trap bars and cheated on me with her behind my back for two months. I realized something strange was going on with us because he started compulsively reading books in English. Then, one morning after breakfast, he told me he was wildly in love with a foreigner. I'm still upset over what happened. And Fabio never spoke to me again, except for in brief, biting emails—cold and lacking affection—in which he would say this was all fate. How he'd found the love of his life, and I'd also soon find my true love… soon. I don't know if I'm trying to torture myself or if it's just that I'm a woman who writes, but I read the articles and poems Samantha publishes online. They're in English, but I understand them because I studied English when I was a kid. She is also a woman who writes, like me. And now that she lives on this side of the world, she's developed an interest in Latin American literature. She recently published a dossier on Bolivian poetry, which, at the end of its introduction, said, "The poets of Bolivia form one small part of a worldwide movement in which nations as we know them disappear, along with progressive 'developmentalist' thinking, to leave only the pure flow of cash, art, and ideas." "The pure flow of cash, art, and ideas..." Now that I think of it, the German company OASE must have had something similar in mind when it built the waterfall of images and text that form over drops of water at the Costanera Center Mall.

I, for one, wasn't thinking about anything in particular when I reached the first floor of H&M, which is where Gary, Eugenia, and I had agreed to meet up. I had the equivalent of 106 dollars in Chilean pesos on me, which I'd taken from my meager savings to spend on clothes. I'm 43, and I make a living teaching poetry workshops in my living room. People sign up for my workshops because they like what I write and think. Sometimes I fantasize about how they think I'm close to poetry. I like thinking that, wherever it may be that poetry exists. "Anybody can write something brilliant," I tell them. "What's hard is connecting with brilliance." And where does poetry exist for women who write? I'm going to confess something that I truly feel bad about. It's a childish sentiment, but it's something that I felt, a feeling that I had and was mine and, therefore, was real. Maybe by putting it into words here, by getting somebody else to read these words-cum-literature, I can manage to rid myself of this terrible feeling and make it vanish. I walked into H&M hoping that the clothes I'd buy would help me get a boyfriend back in Buenos Aires. Now that I'm writing about it, I'm realizing how, all these months my loneliness has made me fantasize about how fashion would save me. The sadness of loneliness made me have such wretched feelings as the thought that dressing well could make somebody love me. And a woman who writes always writes about love. Because if I stop to think, that's the only reason why I was buying clothes there. To find love. Because if there is anything that I don't need, it's more pants, dresses, miniskirts, shoes… More clothes imported from Asia in containers like trunks on ships crossing the South Pacific. Such a beautiful ocean—why must they ruin it with enormous cargo ships filled with gray boxes! Why must the world be like this? It's hard to be a woman who writes. Literature is the most important part of any writer's life—whether a man or a woman. And literature has no body. Words have no colors or shapes. But women writers have to think about dressing like women all the time aside from having to think about our books. We have to make countless minor, strategic decisions about our wardrobe in order to be women. Being a woman is like being a cross dresser. Or worse. Because at least cross dressers can exaggerate. Women cannot. We must be discreet. We must look put together, but it can't be too noticeable… I think about presidents' wives. All the newspapers do is talk about their style. As soon as their husbands take power, hundreds of articles come out about what the first ladies wore to such-and-such event. If the wives of the most powerful men only serve that purpose, what's left for us—the poor, commoner women? For the poor female writers at the vanguard of a war?

But that day, buying clothes was a pretense for getting together with Eugenia and Gary, whom for some reason I hadn't seen in over 7 years. As soon as I spotted them, I realized how much I love them. That they're such incredible humans, filled with goodness and light. And I was grateful to be in that mall, roaming the sales sections with them. Now the clothes faded into the background, becoming merely the excuse for our reunion. The kindling that reignited the flame of our friendship. We tried on everything we thought looked good and asked each other how it fit, giving each other advice, and in the fitting rooms, we each shared everything that had happened in our lives in the years we hadn't seen each other.

"Tonight, we're hosting a poetry reading at the house. We just published a zine with poems by one of your friends. We copied them off her Facebook without asking," Eugenia told me, as I tried on black tights with fluorescent tribal patterns from the sports section. "Do you think she'd mind?"

"Not at all. Why would she be bothered? Quite the contrary, female poets want people to publish them. Furthermore, this friend…" My words trailed off as we heard a deafening siren come off, and confused, people began to run. Everyone dropped their clothes, covering the floor with small blotches of discontinuous colors, not unlike a Cy Twombly painting. I took off my tights as quickly as possible and left the fitting rooms as fast as I could, naked from the waist down. Because I didn't have my shoes on, I realized quickly that the floor was wet, and waves of freezing water quickly rose. There was about to be a flood in the emporium of the democratization of European fashion. There had been an issue with the fountain in the main hall, and water was gushing out of a burst pipe. In Chile, people always say that water is scarce, but in that moment, the eternal snow of the

Andes seemed to have melted all at once just to come through that broken pipe. And not only did H&M's clothes float, but every brand did. The mall, with its cylindrical shape, became a giant washing machine, all the merchandise that was meant to make women feel loved now drifted with the tide in this enormous steel structure. Everything was wet, and the fabric of the pants and dress started to swell and tighten up.

Anybody who didn't make it out in the first 5 minutes (perhaps because they were overwhelmed watching the spectacle or kept looking for their family and friends) now had no choice but to swim to the main entrance. With the water already reaching my waist, it was impossible for me to swim with my clothes on, so I got undressed. Luckily, all I had on was a light skirt, and it was easy to take off. All I had left at this point was my underwear, and I swam the breaststroke to the door. There were a few minutes there where I held my breath and closed my eyes as my mind went blank. Then, with a blank mind, I had a vision. It was my next boyfriend. My next boyfriend didn't have a face, but I could see his hands. They were big, rough hands, and they were sewing. I saw us in my tiny living room, sprawled on the floor, cutting and sewing clothes for me. Countless beautiful articles of clothing made that way. I don't know if I would call them dresses, 'cause they were more like giant bags (but with frills and parts you could add and remove) made of rustic, tattered, opaque fabrics. But they were amazing, because they transformed me into somebody else—a more serious, transparent person. Nothing more opposite from H&M's clothes. That was a perfect day.

Diary of a Cloud Watcher

Dedicated to Juliana Lafitte

I remember, about 8 or 9 years ago, my friend started a blog called *Diary of a Cloud Watcher*. Every day, he wrote about whatever clouds he had seen. And that's it. At the time (maybe because I was mad at my friend over something else), I thought his project was stupid. The idea seemed hackneyed, like something that somebody with nothing to say would do. But now, sitting on a bus as I head to the Atlantic coast, I can't stop staring at the clouds and thinking of adjectives. Earlier, when the day was young yet, the clouds were puffy, like the upper layer of cream on a French or Russian dessert. (I've heard before that Russian pastries are the most sophisticated ones to make in the world.) A thin layer of clouds, stretching across the sky like a woman's voile slip covering her thick legs. Now, they're afternoon clouds, white like hail and sun-kissed. They look like rocks or ships or houses. Below, indifferent to the clouds' milky ways, lies the green of the pampas. Oh, how many times I've dreamed of writing those words. The green of the pampas! The green of the pampas! The green of the pampas! Since I was a little girl, I wanted to find a way to work those words into one of my school essays. But the time wasn't right until today, when, talking about something completely unrelated, at the age of 42, it came to me. What luck! For the pampas pair well with the clouds.

Soon, the fertile land will turn into sand, and I'll reach the sea, over 200 miles away from my house and my painting. Because the same way I'm watching these clouds from a bus on the wide, open highway, I look at a painting when I'm in my three-bedroom apartment in Once. I got it from a painter who is a Capricorn, like me. (Though naming its creator would perhaps detract from the painting, because just as the sky has no author, art shouldn't either.) It's a painting made out of black, gray, and white clay, plus every combination of those three colors you could ever imagine.

It's quite large. It must be three-feet tall. It's hanging across from my bed. I stare at it for hours every day, asking myself if it just might be the best painting in the world, 'cause I can never stop staring at it. It's hard to put into words what it is about this painting or even what it's about, because it's just a thicket of thin strings that fleetingly evoke the roots or branches of a tree. Though in truth, nothing in the painting is really defined. I see different things every time I look at it: the faces of animals or humans, comic-book characters, parts of a house, chunks of trees uprooted by tornados and hurricanes, swirls and feelings.

But art must stay behind, for we're at the beach now, and that's all that matters—the beach and love. Or hatred, both of which are definitely equal in intensity. Though the clouds, you could say, never ever feel hatred. Family time at the beach is the only thing that matters, and the way the clouds decorate the happiness (or unhappiness) of family time at the beach. Yesterday, we visited a park with thermal springs. The hot water shot forth from the earth—a beautiful sensation. At one point, I lay down on a wooden beach chair, and saw that the clouds were identical to the markings on an animal. They were charcoal colored against a dark-gray backdrop. The markings of some type of cow, maybe. Or an elegant crested tinamou. Or a large cat, which, at this time of day, is sleeping peacefully in an African savannah.

Today, Tuesday, January 20th, the clouds decided to go on an excursion and drop down to the sea. That restless foam, driven forth by the wind, was nothing more than small clouds with light, invisible feet.

It's 10 a.m., and I'm sitting on a sand bank. The clouds make me think of the filling of a ski coat or the color of a refrigerator door. Directly in front of me, the clouds are scarce and spongy. To my right, they're forming some kind of mesh or net.

I don't think specific language exists to describe a "net" of clouds. A field of clouds, perhaps? A cloudery? There, to the right, toward Mar de Ajó, the cloudery is denser and less porous.

Music and everything else Earth has could also be compared to clouds. Waves of sound that come and go. In reality, the impulse to write this was the desire to share that what I like about clouds is change. Transformation.

Somebody I know died. He was buried two months ago. Do you think the worms have eaten his body yet? Soon, his bones will be dust, and soon, my bones will be dust too. Will the color of our bones' dust be the same as the clouds? Some day, will my brother's bones and my bones become clouds?

Now, as I drink a coffee at a wooden table in a bar on the only main street in Las Toninas, the edge of the clouds reminds me of the edge of the bubble letters that teenage girls used when they wrote the name of some boy they had liked on the school benches.

I'm lying in the sand. Just now, one cloud looked like a little goat with a viper made of smoke on its head. When I saw it, I felt such joy. The same joy I feel when I see a blue sky. The second I turned around to grab my notebook, the goat disappeared, and all that was left was a lone, asocial cloud with the shape and spirit of a galaxy. But that one faded as well.

It's 6 p.m. There's nothing to do at the beach other than watch the clouds.

I'd like for whoever reads this (if it's ever published) to treat it as a catalog of cloud descriptions for use in novels and short stories. That would be great. I'd love for this text to serve a purpose. I'd love to write a thousand pages about clouds and never write anything else. Obviously, when someone dies, those of us left here on Earth look to the sky. Toward what I think is the east, the clouds are forming waterways with foamy edges and glowing borders.

Later, in the back porch of the house, I take down a wreath. Its beige leaves don't look like clouds. They're something else, broken graphemes from the era of cuneiform. In the afternoon, I realize that the sky and the earth aren't the same thing, though in the mornings when I'm euphoric, I think that they are. The earth is a warm blanket enveloping my brother. I wonder if some part of his body, which has since been transformed into an entity that isn't a body, feels the heat of the sunrays penetrating the ground in some distant, incomprehensible way. My brother was a pioneer of death. The week before he left, when he was at death's door, I had a persistent vision of the darkness of the universe, simultaneously black and luminous, and I felt at peace, for I knew my brother would go to a quiet, beautiful place.

I'm returning to Buenos Aires and admiring the beauty of the pampas. Along the way, cars pass at full speed. It's beautiful to see the windmills, cows, and reeds all yielding to the wind. But it's even lovelier to watch the clouds. This text has become addictive. It's addicting looking for words to describe the clouds above my head. Maybe thinking about clouds is the only way to avoid thinking of death. Now it looks like some clouds escaped to the west where they can try to become pressed flowers.

* * *

I've been back in Buenos Aires for a few days, but soon I will feel an intense melancholy for the coast and the sea. So, I've decided to gather my belongings and take a bus back to Las Toninas. In the city, I don't really get to cloud watch because I live on the ground floor of my building. But one afternoon, as I walked out of the supermarket with bags in both hands, I decided to turn my head up to the sky. And I saw them: a grand tapestry of smoke-colored blots. At that moment, I felt like the clouds were calling me, and I went to an ATM to take out whatever money I had to go back to the sea. Now, the clouds look like the inner part of a stomach—either an animal's or human's, it doesn't really matter. I'm certain this is what intestines must look like. On the other hand, the contrast between the soft waves and the mud-like dark gray crossing over them is wondrous.

I'm at the beach again, and something terrible happened this morning. I was walking back under the sun carrying a plastic bag with a pound of raw meat to make lunch when a group of stray dogs (I'm not sure if I should call them a pack, because there were fewer than five) attacked me. First, a small one that looked like a rat bit my ankle. I screamed in a fit, but no one came to my rescue in this semideserted resort. Then, as I looked for something to defend myself with, a tall one that looked like a monstrous, boar-like Great Dane kicked its hind legs against my shoulders, knocking me over. They wanted the meat in the bag, which I quickly let go off and the four dogs tore apart frenzied. Lying on the dirt ground, on the verge of fainting, I saw how the fibers of the raw meat blended with the light red color of the blood coming out of my ankle.

With my head on the ground, I also saw the clouds, which were like a vast sheet of limestone and air hovering above my suffering.

Then I thought: "The spectacle of the clouds is a hundred times better than the spectacle of blood or anything else of this earth."

Clouds are pure, uncontaminated. Nobody should accuse anybody else ever again of preferring the inconsistency of clouds to the power struggles that are fought beneath them.

ABOUT THE AUTHOR

Cecilia Pavón was born in Mendoza, Argentina, in 1973 and has lived in Buenos Aires since 1992. As co-founder of the independent art gallery, publishing press, and gift shop Belleza y Felicidad, Pavón became a defining figure of the Argentine literary scene in the late 1990s and early 2000s. She also works as a literary translator from English, German, and Portuguese, and translated Chris Kraus, Ariana Reines, and Dorothea Lasky, among others. In 2012, Editorial Mansalva published her collected poetry in *Un hotel con mi nombre* (*A Hotel With My Name*). Her other books of poems include *27 poemas con nombres de persona* (2010), *La crítica de arte* (2016), *Querido libro* (2018), and *La libertad de los bares* (2020). She has also published the short story collections *Los sueños no tienen copyright* (2010), *Pequeño recuento sobre mis faltas* (2015), and *Todos los cuadros que tiré* (2020), as well as an anthology of blog posts titled *Once Sur* (2012). Translations of Pavón's work have been published in English, French, German, and Portuguese.

ABOUT THE TRANSLATOR

Jacob Steinberg was born in Stony Brook, New York, in 1989. He holds a B.A. in Spanish and Latin American Literature from New York University. He has published the poetry collection *Before You Kneels My Silence* (2014). He has translated Cecilia Pavón, CAConrad, and Mario Bellatin, among others. He currently lives in Los angeles.